I'M NOT YOUR OTHER HALF

I'M NOT YOUR OTHER HALF

Caroline B. Cooney

PACER BOOKS

A Member of the Putnam Publishing Group

New York

Published by Pacer Books,
a member of the Putnam Publishing Group
51 Madison Avenue
New York, New York 10010
Copyright © 1984 by Caroline B. Cooney

Designed by Terry Antonicelli
Printed in the United States of America
Third Printing

Library of Congress Cataloging in Publication Data
Cooney, Caroline B.   I'm not your other half.
Summary: A high school junior finds the perfect boyfriend,
only to feel smothered by their constant togetherness.
[1. High schools—Fiction. 2. Schools—Fiction.
3. Friendship—Fictionr I. Title.
PZ7.C7834Im 1984   [Fic]   84-7768
ISBN 0-399-21134-9

For Louisa, Sayre and Harold

I'M NOT YOUR
OTHER HALF

Chapter 1

"Do you believe this?" I said to Annie. We kept laughing instead of talking. We've been telephone freaks for the past eight years, but never did we have a conversation with fewer words and more laughter.

"It's incredible," agreed my best friend. "The last time we discussed life, Fraser, we weren't too impressed."

I twirled my telephone cord like a jumprope. A rhyme I hadn't thought of since Annie and I were nine ran through my head. *Fraser and Michael, sitting in a tree, k, i, s, s, i, n, g.* I giggled again. "Now look at us, Annie. Perfection times two."

But only I had perfection. Annie had gone and fallen for Price, which really *was* incredible, because

Price was the most unsuitable person in all Chapman High. Whereas Michael—nobody could argue that Michael was anything less than perfect.

"Imagine romance beginning with a little boy in horn-rimmed glasses asking for a submachine gun," said Annie. "God works in mysterious ways, Fraser."

All good things in life are better when you can share them with a best friend. Thank you, God, for Annie, I thought. For crazy ideas like Toybrary and little girls like Kit, and most of all for wonderful handsome perfect boys like Michael.

I revised the thought.

It could not be plural. There was only one boy on earth as wonderful as Michael Hollander.

Annie and I were in the library, as we were every Thursday afternoon. We had painted our corner orange, with rainbows soaring to the ceilings, but still, Toybrary was a dark place, and I was often surprised that the children found it so easily.

"The submachine gun has been checked out," I told the little boy. "How about a nice Nerf Ping-Pong ball set?"

The kid was utterly disgusted. Here he came wanting war toys, and this dumb seventeen-year-old girl tried to make him settle for Nerfballs. Annie and I had said many times we should have had a peace-loving toy-lending library, but then we wouldn't have had any little boy patrons. We showed him our war shelf (G.I. Joe, battery-operated tanks, plastic rifles), and for the next half hour Annie and I were stranded in this pile of arms and munitions while an eight-year-old made rifle noises and killed off his enemy.

"Annie?" I said. "Do you ever think a serious mistake has been made? That some other girl is leading the life intended for you?"

Annie was counting sea monsters in a returned Survive game. "Definitely," she said. "God did not mean for me to be stranded at the library loaning out space killer wands."

We laughed, but mostly from habit. Annie and I always laugh together, even when we're depressed. I was relieved when Kit Lipton came in. She was my absolute favorite Toybrary patron: a seven-year-old gap-toothed girl with a passion for Barbie Doll clothing. I helped Kit undo the tiny snaps on a Barbie safari outfit and tried to remember being seven. My second-grade teacher's hoop earrings were always getting caught in her hair. They made me dive off the deep end in swimming class, and I cried. I was a sheep for Hallowe'en, and everybody said *ba-a-a-a, ba-a-a-a,* till I tore off the costume, stuffed it down a toilet and got in trouble with the principal.

Kit sorted through miniature bridal gowns, ice-skating skirts and ski jackets. She was an awkward child, with lopsided brown pigtails and growing-out bangs which eluded the rubber bands. An adult came in for a difficult jigsaw puzzle, and two little boys wanted me to count their returned Legos and verify that all 498 pieces were there.

"I am so thirsty," announced Kit, "that my teeth itch."

Annie laughed and began pouring everybody apple juice. Naturally everybody spilled it, and then everybody fled before I could yell at them. Annie and I were left alone with 498 sticky Legos.

Only half an hour till we close up, I thought gladly. Then I can go home to the really thrilling things in my life—homework; TV reruns; phone calls to organize the fund-raiser.

I was in charge of the appliance booth. Old radios, used blow dryers, unwanted hair curlers.

"If only," I said to Annie, "there could be something in my life sufficiently exciting to make my hair curl."

And at that very moment, during that very thought, something sufficiently exciting walked into my life.

Michael Hollander.

When Annie and I were thirteen, we read nothing but romances. We read one a day, like apples. And if apples keep the doctors away, then romance novels keep the boys away. We went in and out of crushes as if we were charter members of the Crush-of-the-Month Club. But the right boy never came along, and we found early on that we disliked spending time with semi-right boys. Annie and I did everything up to and including making offerings to the Goddess of Love in Annie's gazebo. It's hard to believe now that we felt so romantic about that gazebo. It was a stage, I suppose, when the style of the car means more than arriving at the destination, when the brand of blue jeans is more important than the fit. All we wanted was boys. Our only specification was gender. But once we started dating, we realized that not just any boy would do. He has to have a good sense of humor, we'd tell each other, thus eliminating several hundred of the one thousand five hundred boys in Chapman High. He has to have brains, we'd add—which cut the number down by another several hundred.

One night we were in Annie's gazebo, giddy from the scent of climbing roses and lavendar shrubs, and Annie said to me, "I hope you realize, Fraser, that we have it down to only five boys. And all of those five already have girl friends."

We laughed hysterically, not sure whether it was funny or awful.

Now, on the telephone, we laughed some more, and it was neither hysteria nor grief. It was sheer delight.

We discussed Price (for Annie) and Michael (for me). "The year Michael rode the school bus with us, he was a shrimp," said Annie.

"He's six foot one and a half now," I said. I knew because at Toybrary he stood with his back to the huge flowered How Tall Are You? poster that all our little kids measure themselves on.

"I can't wait for tomorrow," said Annie.

"Michael," I breathed, as if his name were a password to romance.

Most towns the size of Chapman would have two high schools, but we have one, and over three thousand of us attend. My own class has 719. I've lived in Chapman all my life and gone only to public schools, but I don't know a third of the kids in my own class, let alone in the whole school.

Michael was a junior like me, but we had never had a class together. If Michael played on any teams, it wasn't for a sport I went to see. If he was in a club, it wasn't one I had joined. I measured him—six feet one and a half inches high—and I grieved that we had no horizontal measuring stick for the breadth of his shoulders. I was rather surprised I even remembered his name. First and last names—*wow*, lady, I said to myself, staring up from my tiny Toybrary chair. What a memory. So how come you can't zero in on chemistry like that?

"Hi," said Michael, drawing out the syllable to hide the fact that he could not remember our names.

"Hi, Michael," I said. Annie just looked up, her elfin smile sparkling in a cream-complexioned face surrounded by puffs of short dark hair.

"This is my little sister, Katurah," said Michael. "She'd like to check out a toy, if that's okay."

"That's super," I said, and I took my eyes off Michael to look at Katurah. It surprised me that it was quite hard to stop looking at Michael, and it surprised me even more that I had not noticed Katurah. This was due in part to Michael's large frame, and the billowing effect of his huge padded ski vest, but it was also due to Katurah's shyness. She was clinging to his legs. I'd have to peel her off even to look at toys.

"Katurah," I repeated. "That's a lovely name. I like all the sounds in it." I didn't ask her to spell it, because she might not be able to, and we wouldn't exactly win a new patron to Toybrary by publicly humiliating her. One of my first volunteers demanded of kids that they know their right hand from their left in order to use certain toys. Of course, they never could, and they'd flee in embarrassment rather than make the mistake. "I have an unusual name, too, Katurah. My name is Fraser. Fraser MacKendrick. Everybody who hears my name thinks I'm a boy. Every year when school begins,

I have to go down and sign out of boys gym and into girls gym."

I said this to put Katurah at ease, and it worked, because she inched noticeably from behind Michael's leg, but I had not really said it for Katurah. I said it for Michael. I wanted him to know my name. I wanted to get us chatting.

"A shame to change that schedule," remarked Michael. "If you'd stayed in boys gym, it would certainly have livened things up."

I was sitting on a very low chair: a chair meant for people three feet tall, and Michael was still standing. I flashed a smile at him, and he grinned back. The smile stuck on my face. I thought: *I like this boy*. His shoulders were so wide his ski jacket hung awkwardly. I yearned to tug it straight. "Well, Katurah," I said, trying to remember the purpose of Toybrary, "how old are you?"

Katurah clung to Michael's legs and muttered.

"Fine," I said, though I hadn't understood a syllable. "Then you're old enough to check out toys. We're open every Thursday. You borrow any toy you want for two weeks. Use your regular library card."

Katurah peeked out from behind Michael and whispered. Annie and I had been running Toybrary for seven months. It didn't take a mental giant to know what she was saying, because all the little kids her age said it. "That's all right," I said. I'm not really the one with the comforting personality; Annie is. I just copy her technique. "It's easy to get a library card," I explained. "Michael will fill it out for you. Just sign it."

She gulped when I showed her the form. She was thin and wispy, with none of the charm Kit Lipton possessed. Katurah's hair was limp and pale, "straw colored" if you were feeling generous. She looked as if she would grow into the kind of girl that drives me crazy: purposely weak and clinging.

Katurah took the pencil I gave her and laboriously began writing out her name. Her printing was fat and cumbersome, and she ran out of space with two letters left over. "That's okay," I told her to prevent any tears. "Turn the card over and finish your name on the back."

Michael pulled up another tiny chair and sat down next to me. How do you expect me to function with you this close? I thought. But he disregarded my presence entirely and said to his sister, "Nice work, Katurah." It was terrible work, but he seemed honest when he admired it. She smiled at him, and it warmed her face considerably.

Annie got down on the floor with Katurah and began showing her what we had in her age group. Katurah was not interested in her age group. She wanted a calligraphy set, a Scrabble game and a relief-map globe that has a panel board so you can light up the country that interests you.

Michael and I sat a millimeter away, our knees doubled up, our bottoms scarcely fitting on the tiny chairs. It was awkward enough to be funny, and we smiled at each other. Michael said, "You are certainly good with little kids."

"Thank you," I said, although clearly it was Annie who was being good with this particular little kid. I was more in my element with kids Michael's size. I loved organizing Toybrary, and I mildly like running it, but I don't care for the actual pint-size patrons. In winter they always need a Kleenex and in summer they always have mud on their shoes. What I have learned most

16

about Toybrary is that I had better not make a career in day-care nurseries.

"You know, Michael," I said, fishing for information, "I wasn't aware you even had a little sister. I thought you were an only child." I knew nothing whatsoever of Michael's family, but it sounded good.

"This is actually my stepsister," said Michael. Katurah looked up and regarded him solemnly. "My father remarried last year and Katurah came with the package."

He and Katurah exchanged a long look and suddenly I liked both of them a lot more. You could feel in that look a lot of compromises—a decision to make the best of a less-than-perfect situation. In Katurah I saw a maturity that I'd never have suspected, and in Michael a generosity and patience that I found very attractive.

I filled out the library information on the card.

Michael talked about school. I was so interested in what he was saying that it was all I could do not to write "4th period, chemistry, Mr. Bermer" when I meant to enter the phone number.

Of course, Michael was in nothing that I was in. He took some of the same courses, but in a school as large as Chapman, there's quite a selection of chemistry labs and American history classes. He was in Computer Club. I took the required half year of Computer Usage as a sophomore and although I enjoyed it, it certainly didn't inspire me to repeat the experience voluntarily. He was in Cross Country Ski. I detest having cold feet hour after hour.

In Chapman High, it's hard to have overlap unless you plan it. I looked at Michael. The harsh wool of his hunting shirt was almost against my cheek. I thought, Maybe I'll plan a little overlap.

Katurah came over for her library card. "Welcome," I said formally. "I hope we see you every Thursday." *And I hope it's always Michael who brings you.*

"My name is from the Bible," said Katurah solemnly. "What's Fraser from?"

Shy children hardly ever volunteer things that fast. I was quite complimented. And it gave me a chance to inform Michael without making a big deal of it.

"Fraser," I told her, "was my great-great-grandmother's maiden name. My mother came upon it during a genealogy search. She thought it was very attractive, and I was the next child to be born, so I got saddled with it." Actually it had been my father's genealogy stage, but as usual in their relationship, Mom carried out the work. I doubt that my mother would care if all ancient graveyards were turned into parking lots—she just wanted to do whatever Dad was doing.

"My name is boring," said Michael. "But I like Fraser. How come your mother didn't name you by your great-great-grandmother's first name instead?"

"Because her first name was Viola Maude. Even my mother realized that it would be hard to go through life in contemporary America with a name like Viola Maude."

"Viola Maude," whispered Katurah. "I love that name, Fraser. If I get a new doll for Christmas, I'm going to call her Viola Maude."

Michael teased her gently about Christmas and Santa and the odds on getting a doll that could be named Viola Maude. I could not take my eyes off his sweet smile and his firm features. He had a longish nose, a rather dramatic profile for a soft-spoken person.

18

I have hazel eyes, but last year I got green-tinted contact lenses. It makes my eyes startlingly bright, a green not found in nature. Although I like it (and I love contacts; they make me feel so much prettier than my old glasses), I'm sometimes embarrassed by my eyes.

Michael glanced at me, and suddenly I felt like a doll named Viola Maude, a porcelain doll with eyes too green, staring glassily out from behind too-long black eyelashes.

I began blushing. Must look like a Christmas tree, I thought. Scarlet and green.

Michael said, "Are you going to the football game on the chartered bus Saturday?"

Our high school sends a great many graduates on to State, and there's quite a strong State following. Each home football game, the high school charters a bus. You can sign up for the season or for a single game. I don't care enough for football to bother with the whole season, but Annie and I always go once. We had, indeed, chosen this Saturday. "Yes, I am," I told him.

Michael smiled again, and I drowned in the smile, but he didn't notice. He stood up, taking Katurah's hand. "That'll be nice," he said. "I'll see you there. Thanks for helping my sister."

"You're welcome," I said.

"Goodbye, Fraser." He said it nicely, with the *zh* sound I use, instead of the *z*. *Frazhure*. It's softer that way, less demanding of a person who expected you to be named Susan or Kimberley.

A little girl took home a Noisy Number Robot Electronic Teacher, and a little boy went for a Rough Rider Impossible Super Devil Roadway Loop, and then it was time to close up. Annie was laughing a rippling chuckle that kept on going, like a brook. "Do you have a problem?" I said mildly.

"No. You do. Your crush is developing like a car at the Indianapolis Speedway, Fraser. Zero to one hundred in sixty seconds."

"You know," she said over the phone, "I was jealous that night."

"You *were*?" Impossible to imagine Annie having unpleasant thoughts about me or anyone else. "It didn't show."

"I could just see you with the perfect boy. Off you'd go, dancing down the sand, your honey hair flying in the breeze, your hand in his, laughing together. I'd be stranded there without a boy. Alone and cold."

I shivered slightly before I laughed it off. More than once, the same scene had appeared in my mind. About our friendship and what could happen to it if one of us started dating and the other did not. All those offerings in the gazebo paid off, I thought. We've not only started dating terrific boys—we're *double* dating them.

"We," said Annie contentedly, "will be chapter nine of every paperback romance we ever read. Where the laughing foursome sits in the booth at the ice-cream parlor, their heads close together. There's always a photograph like that in the yearbook."

Annie and I talked till nearly midnight, while I twirled the cord and jumped mentally. *Fraser and Michael, sitting in a tree, k, i, s, s, i, n, g.*

As surely as spring follows winter, I thought, life will be better for having the boys in it. Annie and I will be like flowers in the sun, full of color and joy.

I did not remember then that not all flowers bloom at once. Some of them fade and die.

20

Chapter 2

Saturday was cold. The thermometer was in the high teens when we assembled at the school to get on the bus. Presumably there was a sun in the sky, but it seemed very far away. In another galaxy, perhaps. The sky was the color of lint—white, gray and limp. The wind came in gusts and penetrated to the marrow of our bones.

The front of Chapman High is beautiful—three stories of brick, with immense stone columns and finely proportioned stone steps. Unfortunately, buses load in the back, where there are no rows of softly swaying hemlocks, no gentle brick walls, no delicate tracery of birch and dogwood. Just a parking lot, a row of dumpsters and a generator in a wire enclosure. The pavement is pockmarked from last winter's frost heaves, and pieces of newspaper blow in the wind.

I had brought along a fat old quilt, and Annie had a holey old Army blanket. I wanted to wrap up in my quilt right out there in the parking lot, but pride prevented me. Pride also prevented me from putting on my tie hat. My ears get cold easily, and I still get the ear infections that other people outgrew when they were four years old. In windy cold weather I can either wear a hat that covers my ears, or I can make an appointment with my doctor.

The hat that works for me is plain gray wool, with a soft flannel liner, that hangs in two long fat ribbons like the ears of a very tired bunny. The ties loop under my chin, and I feel stupid and matronly wearing it. But I've tried everything else. Ear muffs slip off; ear flaps aren't tight enough; scarves are too thick to tie under the chin.

There was no way I would have Michael's first judgment of me include the gray bunny hat, so I was standing there with my ears turning red, wishing he would hurry up so I could make a good impression on him and *then* put on the hat.

The bus arrived.

Not the usual stylish one with corduroy upholstery and its own bathroom. A regular yellow school bus. Annie moaned. "For this we paid good money? Lumps and cold vinyl? We won't drive to the University. We'll lurch."

I was too cold for a wisecrack about the resemblance to her own driving. The fillings in my teeth hurt whenever I opened my mouth. I was resigned to the school bus. School inures you to certain forms of torture.

22

Annie hopped up and down as the cold moved through her sneakers. She was wearing flannel-lined jeans with the extra turns to compensate for her lack of height, and she had thick fuzzy ankles of red plaid. Her shirt was red wool, over a red-heart-dotted turtleneck, and her ski jacket was electric blue. I was almost entirely in green, with a few scraps of white to offset it. We were a very colorful pair.

I had washed my hair twice (the first time I blew it dry, it came out in peculiar stiff tendrils), and when I left the house, it was hanging in soft, lightly tucked waves, but now the wind had snarled and matted it. Hurry up, Michael, I thought.

I shifted the picnic case. Thick, padded, soft vinyl, filled with yummy food and four soft drinks.

"We should have brought a thermos of something hot instead," said Annie, shivering violently. "How much do we really want to go to this football game anyhow?"

"A lot," I told her.

Annie grinned. Her tiny even teeth gleamed. Both of us had worn braces for years. We always notice teeth, because we respect the pain involved acquiring good ones. "We might as well board. If we don't get seats now we'll end up having to sit over the wheels." We shuffled toward the bus.

"Can't be that heavy," said Michael's teasing voice.

Even before I lifted my eyes, my heart lifted. It was as though the heavy, somber cold of the day had vanished, and we were somewhere in Bermuda—white sand, blue sky, soft warm sun and all the hours on earth to spare.

"We're heavy eaters," I told him.

Michael looked unconvinced. "You?" he said, nodding his chin at my slim legs. All of me is slim, which is fine if it's ankles, less so if it's shoulders and chest. My face is narrow too, but I like to think it's elegant, especially the new way I'm wearing my hair, swept back like combed honey.

Michael took the picnic carrier from me and held it up with one finger.

"Show off," I said. "Fitness freak."

We grinned at each other.

"Hi, there, Fraser," said another voice. "Hi, Annie."

Standing next to Michael was Price Quincy. It was all I could do not to say, "Oh, shit. You." I bit back the words. Annie was saying, "Why, Price, great to see you" and so I said, "Price, how've you been?" trying not to sound gloomy.

I did not care how Price had been and I hoped he would not tell us. Price is a reasonably attractive person in the flesh and in some ways in the personality. But he's wild in that borderline way that makes me nervous. No thought of consequences. No concern for people. Just doing whatever is exciting at the moment.

Some girls are very attracted to that. They like the idea of a guy having a six-pack and then driving over the school field doing wheelies. I can only think, Yes, and what if you go home and take the curve at the bottom of Chapel Street at fifty miles an hour and some little kid like Kit Lipton happens to be crossing the street?

"You were smart to bring food," said Price. "Saves money."

24

"Mostly it saves time," said Annie. "My time is too valuable to waste standing in line."

Price laughed, his eyes on Annie. Now, I certainly check boys out, and I certainly think Annie is a girl worth checking out, but it's different when you actually watch the eyeballs trace the body and you know they're wishing for no fabric between them and the full nude view. I felt slightly sick and turned to see how Michael was looking at me.

He wasn't. He was looking at the bus.

Thanks a lot, I thought indignantly. I mean, you could at least show a *little* interest.

"I knew I should have brought a thicker coat," he said. "I always need padding on those buses."

"We brought two blankets," I told him. "We re-upholster any bus we ride in. You want to share?"

There was the briefest of pauses, as if we were all calculating something on invisible calculators. Price said, "How about Annie and I take the Army blanket there and you and Michael take the—whatever that thing is."

"This is a Depression quilt," I informed Price stiffly. "It is an honor to sit on it, so it's just as well you realized you deserve only an old Army blanket in standard olive drab."

"A Depression quilt?" repeated Price. The quilt was ugly, in fat blocks of dark brown, striped gray and rusty black. "Is it supposed to start up your depression or clear it?" he asked.

"This quilt," I said, "was made by my great-grandmother during the Depression out of old worn-out men's suits in the church charity box. It's stuffed with pieces of old coats and it wasn't meant to be pretty. It was meant to keep them warm when they couldn't afford to heat the bedrooms."

Michael looked at it with genuine interest. Price shrugged and led Annie onto the bus to reserve seats. What a sacrifice for Annie, I thought, having to share Price's company. "Your great-grandmother," said Michael. "That would be Viola Maude Fraser's daughter?"

I was immeasurably delighted. Of course it was only two days, and Michael didn't have a wind cavern behind his eyes. But it was quite a compliment, his keeping track of my ancestry.

Price and Annie were five seats behind the driver. It took me one step to pass them to slip into the sixth seat; one second was all I had to look at Price and Annie; and one moment was all I needed. They were framed in that curious way couples have. Heads coming together, slightly bowed, the same sort of intimacy of hands about to touch.

Oh, no, I thought. Oh, Annie, don't fall for Price Quincy, please.

I would have worried, but Michael sat next to me, and I forgot Annie. They were inches from us; we could easily have addressed them over the seat back, but we never even thought of them. We talked of ordinary things, mostly school, yet the conversation was intense. It was intimacy with a pause. I was considering each syllable before I uttered it. Saying to myself, Yes, I'll be that honest; it's safe.

With Annie, everything simply poured out.

Someday, Michael and I will know each other well enough that we won't stop to deliberate, I thought. There will be no walls between us.

26

I was astonished when we arrived at State: I had not noticed a single spine-splitting pothole, a single red light.

Oh, Fraser MacKendrick, I thought, as Michael and I got up and he folded the Depression quilt over his arm and stood back to let me out of the seat. Have you got it bad!

The bleachers at State are stone, set into the hillside like an ancient Greek stadium. The wind came through the goal posts and tore cruelly up the stone stands and through our clothing. I had no choice. I took my crumpled sagging old gray wool hat out of my jacket pocket.

"What's that?" said Michael. "It looks like a litter of gray mice."

Annie giggled. "It's her bunny hat, Michael. Fray has tender ears."

Michael looked at my ears with interest. It was the first time my ears had ever served a better purpose than providing holes for my earrings. "I don't know about tender," he said, "but they sure are red." He took the hat from my stiff fingers and fluffed it out, sticking his fist inside for a model head. "Wild!" he said, laughing. "Where did you get this? It's so old-fashioned." He put it on me, accidently bending my ears forward. I reached up to unfold them, and our hands touched: frozen flesh against frozen flesh. The vapor from our warm laughter rose up between us.

"That reminds me of a shower at my house," said Michael.

"What, you don't have hot water?" I exclaimed. "How Spartan."

"We have hot water. We just don't have water pressure. We don't even call it a shower. We call it a mist. As in, *'Michael, are you out of the mist yet?'*"

Not too far from us, two teams were playing football, and around us people shouted and cheered, but among the four of us, there was just talk and touching and laughter. Wouldn't it be incredible, I thought, if both Annie and I found the right boys at the same time, in each other's company? Could anything on earth be finer than both of us becoming couples at the same moment? I struggled to like Price, but clearly this was easier for Annie than for me.

"Let's have something hot to eat," said Price. "My treat, Annie. French fries, cheeseburgers, fried onions and hot chocolate. Okay?"

"Wonderful," agreed Annie, although she hates fried onions even if it's somebody else eating them. She doesn't like hot chocolate either and has had coffee every morning since she was very little (which may have been a contributing factor to her height).

"That means you and I get roast beef on hard rolls," I told Michael. "Also bananas and pickles."

"Bananas and pickles," said Michael. "My favorite combination."

I was warm only on my left side, from my knee to my shoulder, where Michael and I were leaning against each other. "This is like trying to get warm in front of a fireplace," I said.

"Try my lap."

I slid onto his lap. It was a perfect fit. I am tall, but Michael is taller. I could actually snuggle against him. I loved it.

I was aware of every inch of him—his wide-wale

cords, the frayed belt strung through the loops, the pale-gray striped oxford shirt under the heavy gray hand-knit sweater.

I turned my head to rest against him, and Annie was nodding at me, a secret smile on her lips. In the air she traced a shape. Another person might think it was a smile, or a crescent moon. I knew it was a watermelon.

Chapter 3

"**M**om?" I said at breakfast. I was now three days, or seventy-two hours, into my crush on Michael. "Would it be all right if I took the car today?" I handed her a plate of buttered whole-wheat toast with bacon and a sliced banana.

My mother is flustered at breakfast. She is not a morning person, and having to be well-dressed, well-groomed and well-fed, all before seven-thirty, looms large five mornings a week.

She eyed the clock. "I guess so. But that means you'll have to drive me first and come back to drive your father. And pick us up in reverse order. Honestly, I wish we had two cars. If we weren't saving for your college . . . Oh, dear, Fraser, look at this button hanging by one thread. Now I'll have to change my blouse."

She kicked off her high heels for more running speed and dashed up to her room to get another blouse.

My father, who sits quietly in the corner of the breakfast room until poor Mom has fled the premises, sipped his coffee. "Why do you want the car, honey? It's so much trouble."

Because I need more than eighteen seconds after my last class. Because I intend to drift down the hall and find Michael Hollander. Because I want to be able to go somewhere with him, instead of race like a rabbit for the bus.

"Because I have to work on my botany lab project after school," I said.

My father is very proud of my lab project. Twice he's gone to school to discuss it with my teacher. I am the only student taking both chemistry and botany, and my father daydreams more about my future than I do. I don't have the slightest idea what my future is going to be, but every day Dad comes up with a new possibility. Actually I took two sciences mostly to get them over with, but he is convinced he has a future Nobel Prize-winner on his hands. "Oh, well," he said happily. "In that case, drive your mother and I'll walk down to Chapel Street and catch the commuter bus so you don't have to drive me as well."

I felt a stab of guilt, but it wasn't much of a stab. More of a paper cut. Michael seemed to have come right into the breakfast room with us filling the very air with his desirable presence, and he was all that mattered.

Of course, when I arrived at the school lot after dropping Mom off, every single slot was filled. I had to drive all the way down Buckley to find a parallel parking space, and then run back five blocks over patches of ice where last night's drizzle had frozen in the dawn cold, and I was late to homeroom.

One of the advantages to being a star student is that you never get into trouble. Your teachers automatically assume that you were doing something of vital importance, like inoculating your corn with nitrogen-fixing blue-green algae. Sure enough, nobody said a word.

I had thought last week of going for a few long country walks after school. If I followed the meadow path in back of the yards of Coventry Road, I could scout out wild grapevine and bittersweet that clung to the trees along the meadow rim. My master plan for Christmas included making bittersweet wreaths for all my Christmas presents. Gray-brown vines with the bright piercing orange and scarlet berries and perhaps a bright calico ribbon. I could store them in the garage on the rafter nails until December tenth or so, and then give them out.

Was Michael the gathering-bittersweet type?

If the opportunity came up for me to suggest a date, what would I say? A movie? A meal? A walk down Coventry meadow path?

If he wasn't the type, I would not bother. I would buy everybody something at the gift shop instead.

After school I dawdled to my locker. There was no way for Michael to know which of the three thousand lockers in school was mine. I detested Chapman High for being so large. In any decent small school a few turns around a central hall and you would have located anybody. But I could wander the halls of Chapman for two hours and still not encounter Michael Hollander.

When fifteen minutes passed without a trace of Michael (Come now, Fraser, I thought, a trace? What did you expect? The lingering scent of his aftershave to guide you?), I went down to work on my corn after all.

Ah, the Goddess of Love and Crushes.

She had directed Michael to the botany lab, and he was just leaving, looking sorrowful—because I wasn't there.

"Hi, Michael."

His head turned, his eyes lit on me, his lips moved into a smile. "Hi, Fraser."

We were locked in appreciation of each other, and we laughed slightly, like children, linking hands and walking instinctively toward the parking lot. Michael, evidently sharing all my thoughts, had driven *his* father's car.

There is nothing, *nothing*, more awkward than two people in love driving separate cars.

We got into Michael's car in the student lot (he had arrived early) and drove five blocks down Buckley where I hopped out, got into my car, and followed him across town to Vinnie's.

McDonald's, Burger King, Wendy's, Roy Rogers and Arby's all have their place in my life (I am a dedicated hamburger hound), but Vinnie's booths have high walls blackened with years of initials—dark, quiet corners where you can sit in peace for hours.

"So," said Michael, "tell me about blue-green algae."

"It's not exciting. We've got six varieties of blue-green algae in a water solution and we inoculate the soil around the corn, testing for the best fertilizer. The real problem is keeping the algae alive. I'm working on various nutrients to add to the water solution. Karen de

33

Forio is changing the algae types and Lisa Schmidt is monitoring the other variables, like sun and heat. We're going to exhibit at the state Science Fair this winter."

"You like laboratory research?"

"Not really. I liked coming up with the theory, and I liked figuring out how to approach it, but I can't say I actually like doing it."

"Same as Toybrary," said Michael.

I stared at him. "How do you know I don't enjoy Toybrary?"

"Just a guess. You were wonderful with Katurah, but somehow I don't see you happily on your hands and knees playing with little kids."

He had thought about me. Tried to analyze me.

He changed the subject to one clearly dearer to his heart than Toybrary. His basement. Cellars do not interest me, but Michael's was full of his electronic equipment, from Betamax to police scanner, from microcomputer to electronic keyboard. There was no way I was going to interrupt our first date together by saying that cellars and electronics bored me equally, so I said things like, "Oh, I'd love to see that" and "Oh, Michael, you have to demonstrate that for me."

He even told me about his father's remarriage. "It surprised me," said Michael. "Dad was so crushed when Mom divorced him. He said he'd never have a woman in his life again. And there he was, six months later, beaming, laughing, his arm around Judith, phoning the church to set up the wedding."

"What did you think about it?" I said.

He shrugged. "It was hard to have any opinion at all. It never happened to me before. All of a sudden, there we were. This entirely different family, occupying different rooms, having to get along."

We talked about Judith and Katurah and his father. His mother seemed very shadowy. It gave me a quiver to talk about divorce, as though just talking about it could make it happen in my own family. My parents? My brother Ben and and his wife, Lynn? I changed the subject almost superstitiously and told Michael about Coventry Road and the meadow path that wound among the grape vines and the bittersweet tangles.

"Very poetic," he said. "If it had snow on it, I might ski on the path, but woods have no appeal for me otherwise."

Well, so much for that, I thought, mentally crossing it off my list of possibilities. I tried not to think about skiing. My coordination reaches its limits with walking. Besides, I can't afford skiing. The trouble with so many activities is they cost so much. When Ben wanted to have a sailboat, that was it; they couldn't afford anything else. It was a good thing Lynn was willing to take up boating too.

"Tell me about your family," said Michael.

"Ordinary," I said, but that was not my opinion at all. I thought my family was wonderful and interesting. I'm backing off, I thought. This is our first date. I can't start out by hiding myself. That's no way to be a couple, faking things.

"Impossible," said Michael. "I saw you on the Good Morning Show talking about Toybrary, and you were extraordinary. You were wearing some blue shirt and asking for donations of unusual toys. I made up my mind right then I wanted to get to know you."

35

Michael had not come into the library to show Katurah how Toybrary worked. He had brought Katurah for an excuse. To meet *me*.

For this boy, I thought, staring at his soft dark hair and his bright eager eyes—eager because of me—for this boy, I believe I could learn to love electronics and skiing.

It was impossible to pay attention during dinner that night. I was far too wrapped up in my thoughts of Michael and me.

My brother, Benjamin, and his wife, Lynn, were over. Ordinarily I love their company. I like to hold my nephew Jake (though it seems to me that parents who spent nine months thinking up names could do better than *Jake*). And I like having coffee afterward. Dad and Ben can't bear sitting at the table after the eating is done, so Mom and Lynn and I sit there for hours. Sometimes Mom talks about work, and Lynn talks about missing work, and Mom talks about childbirth and Lynn talks about sailing.

Lynn didn't even know what a sailboat was before she married Ben. Actually, she was afraid of the water. But Ben's interests pretty much center around boats, navigation and weather. So, before long, Lynn's did too. She adopted Ben's hobbies the way other couples adopt children.

Lynn had brought a hot casserole, and we were eating in the dining room for a change. There's an aesthetic pleasure to that room the other rooms lack. Several years ago, Mom joined Needle N Thread, which meets the second and fourth Wednesday of every month. Each year the club does a different kind of needlework together. The first year was crewel embroidery, so our dining-room curtains have a Jacobean flavor. The next year, needlepoint, so all eight chairs have magnificent cushions, three of which Mom designed herself. The year after that was knit lace. The ecru tablecloth looks like something a Colonial governor's wife might have.

Mom went back to work when Ben was a sophomore at college. She asked for a typing job at a blue-jeans manufacturer, but they hired her to run the office for the marketing research team. About six months ago she stopped running the office and joined the team itself. The chief result, aside from more money and prestige, is that she's far more tired. If she didn't have her needlework, I don't know what she'd do. It's her lifeline. Every night she thanks God for dishwashers, disposals, clothes dryers and electric hair curlers and sits down with the latest needlework project.

"So how were blue jeans today, Mom?" said my brother.

"We're getting ripped off around the globe. People reproduce shoddy third-rate jeans with *our* brand names and . . ."

Usually I follow Mom's stories with interest, because I'm so proud of her—carving out this career— and because the blue-jeans industry fascinates me, but tonight all I could think of was Michael. Michael's shoulders and Michael's muscles. Michael's eyes and Michael's height.

"So, Fray," said my brother. "How's your love life?"

I blushed scarlet.

"That good, huh? Just don't get in over your head, kiddo."

My father snorted. "It's difficult to imagine Fraser getting in over her head. When I was her age, I had the maturity of a tomato in April. Fraser arrived mature on the vine."

Lynn said she thought Jake was getting a tooth.

Ben said traffic was bad because of road repair.

Daddy said that although casseroles were good and he was grateful to Lynn for making such a tasty one, he preferred steak.

Mom and Ben spent ten minutes smoothing that little remark over, and I spent ten minutes thinking about Michael. I planned my entire wardrobe for the next week around what Michael might or might not like. This is ridiculous, I thought. I don't see him in school. He doesn't see me either.

My green chamois shirt, I thought. Over what? My turtleneck with the green hearts? My sweater with the rainbow stripes against the white background?

"So what's the latest project in Needle N Thread?" said Lynn.

"Oh, I'm not in the club any longer," said my mother.

I choked on some tuna in the casserole, and my father nodded, as if he had known this was what happened when you had casserole instead of steak, and he whacked me on the back. "Why not, Mom?" I managed at last.

"It meets Wednesday. And now that your father is no longer keeping the pharmacy open on Wednesdays, I'd rather be home with him."

I could not believe it. I absolutely could not believe it. She was giving up her club just because Dad was going to be home watching television? Unreal.

I thought, if I wear the chamois shirt tomorrow, then I can wear my blouse with the lace cuffs the day after that. I guess you dress up for a crush whether the recipient attends the occasion or not.

Lynn said that she and Ben were taking up jogging. Maybe Michael and I will take up dancing, I thought. I saw myself wearing a long, lovely gown, with a fitted satin bodice to show off my thin waist. Michael, his arm around me, would . . .

Ridiculous. The only dances at Chapman High feature rock bands, and everybody wears jeans.

Still, Michael and I would do everything together. Like Ben and Lynn, or my mother and father. It would be perfect.

Suddenly I had to talk to Annie. Sometimes I think I know what a craving for drugs or alcohol must be like, because when the desire to talk privately to Annie hits, nothing else will do. I can't even speak to other people, even if they're my parents and brother, because only Annie will understand.

"Excuse me," I said. "I have to phone Annie."

I ran to the privacy of my room, dialed the number I literally know better than my own, because I've dialed it so many hundreds of times, and sighed with pleasure when Annie said hello.

Annie lives farther down Coventry Road, in a romantic turreted Victorian Painted Lady, a mansion painted gold with rose-beige trim, brown outlines and vermillion accents. Even the yard is romantic, sloping down through a bank of laurel, opening onto a smooth emerald-green lawn wrapped in white birches. A little stone path flanked by short lavender shrubs leads to a delicate wood-laced gazebo, vined with Climbing Blaze roses and topped with a flying-angel weathervane.

I was nine and Annie was nine and a half when she moved there. My nine-year-old attitude was that it would be okay to have another girl on Coventry Road, but it would be wonderful to play in that gazebo at last. The previous owners didn't let kids on their property. So it was with high hopes that I went to meet this Annie Walpole, only to find that wasps nested in her gazebo. I was utterly disgusted. Anyone who kept wasps in her gazebo was no friend of mine. Anyhow, my cousin Hank was coming for a month that summer so I didn't need Annie.

My mother felt otherwise. "You need a best friend."

"When school starts in September, I'll look for one," I promised.

"Annie is here now. You're both just drifting around this summer and I want you to get acquainted. Life can't be savored to its fullest without a good friend."

"*You* don't have a best girl friend," I pointed out. My mother's old college friends were always calling her up, and she was always claiming she couldn't go; she was doing something with Dad.

"That's different," she said. "I have your father."

I felt my cousin Hank could be my best friend, but Mother insisted my best friend was going to be a girl, and the girl was going to be Annie Walpole.

It was a point of honor to resist.

Mom and Mrs. Walpole signed Annie and me up for swimming lessons. I cleverly refused to float at Registration and thereby got into Beginners Class while Annie was in Intermediate. Mrs. Walpole sent us down to the corner on errands, but I divided the list and sent Annie to the grocery while I handled the drugstore. Mother even took us to the movies every weekend (a blissful state never to be repeated). However I sat on Mom's left and Annie sat on her right and the only conversation we had was whether somebody wanted the rest of my Jujubes because I was full.

Late in August, after Hank had gone home and before school started, during those hot drowsy days when life seems to have come to a pleasant, if sweaty, halt, my brother Ben brought home an enormous watermelon. Annie and I rolled that watermelon all the way down Coventry Road to her house because Annie refused to sit on our steps to eat it since our steps were blistering in the hot sun. *Her* steps, she said, were in the shade. And *your* steps, I said, are within striking range of your wasps.

"Chicken," she said.

"Jerk," I told her.

We sat on Annie's back steps and chopped the watermelon with a huge shiny meat cleaver that Mrs. Walpole would never have let us touch if she had been home. For some reason we agreed to eat the entire watermelon and we consumed that melon with a barbaric speed that made the juice dribble down our chins and attracted every stinging insect on Coventry Road.

"If they sting me, I'm killing you, Annie Walpole," I said, and I spit a flat black seed like a bullet against her. I can spit farther than *that*, she said scornfully, and she began a rapid-fire attack on her garage wall.

We must have spit a thousand seeds that afternoon, and the bees dodged and hummed and the wasps covered the half moons of green and white rind that we had dropped all over the steps, and neither of us got stung even once.

Which was how Annie and I became friends.

I never see a watermelon without thinking of Annie. Once in eighth grade, I tried to write an essay about it for English. I got the words down, and they expressed what I wanted to say, but it felt like a trespass. How could I expose our friendship for Mr. Hahn to red-pencil and grade? So I wrote about autumn instead: cider and thick jackets and the kick-crunch of leaves in the street.

Annie and I took up watermelon collecting. We made quilted watermelon tote bags and needlepoint watermelon glasses cases. We painted watermelons in oil for our bedroom walls and rimmed our mirrors with watermelon stickers. We made watermelon wishes the way other people wished on first stars, or first Mondays.

"It's midnight," said Annie regretfully. "I suppose we should hang up."

"We really have said everything there is to say," I admitted.

"The forecast tomorrow is for chilly winds," said Annie. "But, Fraser, it's definitely going to be a watermelon day again."

Chapter 4

Michael stared at me in amazement. He was still so new to me that I hadn't seen all his expressions yet. I loved the look of him surprised—the way his eyebrows lifted and his head tilted. "Pick up a log cabin?" Michael repeated dubiously.

"Some date," observed Price. "Picking up a log cabin."

"It comes in sections," I said reassuringly. "Bolted together. Once we dismantle it, we should be able to lift it easily."

The boys looked nervous. "Fraser," said Michael, "I'm a weight lifter, and I'd be hard-pressed to pick up a log cabin."

I laughed at his pun, and he grinned back, glad I got the joke. He didn't grin long, though, because he was afraid I was serious about carrying this log cabin around. I could tell he was thinking that either he strained his back and got a hernia, or else he ruined our budding romance by explaining that normal high-school kids did not go around picking up log cabins for fun. I would have kidded the boys along until we got to Cinnamon Ridge, but Annie—typically—couldn't hold back. "It's really just a playhouse," she explained. "Mr. Harte's children outgrew it, and he's donating it to Toybrary as long as we haul it off."

Michael was visibly relieved.

"That's why we need you, Price," said Annie sweetly. "My car died, and I love you for your van."

Price laughed. Annie looked adoringly up at him. Price, being Price, had serious objections to the whole plan. "What kid would want to borrow a cabin?" he said. "I can see a kid borrowing Lincoln Logs or a G.I. Joe set. But a *cabin*? You two girls are being had. The only thing this guy Harte wants is free garbage removal."

"I don't know," said Michael reflectively. One of the things I already liked about him was the way he considered everything that came up, instead of waving it off instantly, like Price. "My little sister would love a log cabin. Two weeks of playing pioneer. Brave settler woman. I think a log cabin will be a real hit."

Praise God for little sisters like that, I thought. I'd never have met Michael if it wasn't for his little sister.

Price shrugged. "Okay. Let's roll."

Cinnamon Ridge was a subdivision cut into the woods—a wilderness of thin gray trunks punctuated by large dark-red, dark-blue or dark- brown houses. At the appointed hour we curved up the driveway that said Harte on the mailbox. But the house was locked, the lights off, the garage empty. We stood uncertainly next to the van, feeling like trespassers, but there in the backyard was undoubtedly the playhouse we had come to get.

"I always wanted a yard with boulders like this," said Michael. "So I could ambush people and leap off speeding horses and shoot arrows from behind thick tree trunks."

We walked down a narrow path to the tiny clearing where the playhouse was tucked—indeed as if desperate settlers had wearily carved their space in the unknown. Michael and I led. Price and Annie followed. In only three double dates we had fallen into a pattern. Annie talked to Price, I talked to Michael, the four of us talked together. But Annie and I did not talk to each other. I had a sense that we should reserve our private conversations for later, that after all, we could talk to each other any time. But it was most odd to be with Annie, from whom I had been inseparable for eight years, and not be constantly turning to tell her something. I had to train myself to tell Michael instead. "Did you ever have that yard?" I asked.

"No. Just a metal swing and a sandbox."

It took all Michael's strength to loosen the rusted bolts. His knuckles turned white, and sweat appeared on his forehead. I loved watching him and he loved showing off. Annie and I could not have done it without him, and he knew it. I guess Price felt his van wasn't an equal gift to Michael's strength, so he began carrying the log sections by himself back to the van, resisting any help from us. Annie put the hardware in a little box and wrote directions for reassembly on the lid. I just stood there, feeling cold, vaguely watching distant neighbors put more birdseed in their feeders and in-

45

tently watching Michael work. "I guess that's it," said Michael at last.

You think you know your best friend. I knew that Annie's opinion of cheerleaders was close to her opinion of homework assignments—very, very low; Annie often told me that football games would be improved by chamber music at half time—but Annie suddenly burst into a cheer.

"Yay, rah rah, *Michael!*" she shrieked, leaping into the air and waving a brown-leafed branch for a pom-pon. I gaped at her, too astonished to be embarrassed for her. She looked less like a cheerleader and more like a frantic penguin. "Let's have a cheer for *Price!*" she screamed. "Give me a *P!*"

I could not possibly have participated in her cheer; I was rooted to the spot with humiliation for both of us, but Price promptly jumped up on a big gray rock glittering with mica and bellowed, "*P!*"

"Give me an *R!*" Annie yelled, twirling around him.

Michael and I looked at each other, and the fact that he was as astonished as I made me laugh, and then we both laughed, and we yelled with Price, "R!" The first yell got rid of my inhibitions. The four of us vaulted crazily around the tiny clearing, whooping and hollering like drunken pagans. Price began a chain dance. He put Annie's hands on his waist, Michael put my hands on Annie's, and Michael gripped me. We wound around the woods, tooting like toy trains.

It was at this moment that the police car came up the driveway.

I have never felt so stupid in my life. We paused in our train movements like little children playing freeze tag. Two policemen got out of the car. "The neighbors called," said the taller one grimly. "They told us a bunch of hooligans were destroying property up here."

Our hands dropped from each other's waists. Michael folded his arms across his chest, removing himself from me and our horseplay. Price stood stiff and furious, his whole posture one of seething anger, as if the police were trespassing on him instead of us on the Harte property. But Annie, still exhilarated from her cheering, gave the police her impish smile. "Nonsense," she said, giggling. "We represent Toybrary and we're picking up a log cabin."

Never had the word "Toybrary" sounded more unlikely. I should have called it Library Toy Lending Service, I thought.

Annie—still dancing, grinning like a devil at Price—looked high on drugs even to me. "We really do run a volunteer group called Toybrary," I said desperately. "Mr. Harte said we could have this cabin."

The policemen stared at me expressionlessly. My eyes are too green, I thought. It's probably a sign of drug abuse.

"Identification, please," said one, taking out his notebook. It was a cheap spiral bound notebook, the kind you write class assignments in. It horrified me. The thought of my name, my address, my driver's license number written down permanently in that notebook was nauseating. Beside me, Michael sucked in his breath, and Price muttered curses to himself. The officers were not hard of hearing. They turned to Price, as the most obviously hostile of the group, and asked for his identification first.

Price looked at them with loathing. "No," he said flatly.

I stared at Price with disbelief. Why, oh why, had Annie taken up with a kid whose acquaintance with cops went beyond an elementary-school safety assembly?

Annie said, "Now, Price, relax. Any minute now Mr. Harte will drive up the lane and this will all be settled. Show the man your driver's license."

And Price relaxed. Because Annie told him to. I marveled.

Sure enough, Mr. Harte arrived moments later, full of apologies, grateful to the police for being such magnificent guardians of the peace, and sparing me the horror of having my own name written down. And as we were driving off, Mr. Harte even handed me a check for fifty dollars. "For Toybrary," he said, smiling. "It's such a fine idea and I want you to stock up on interesting things for children to borrow."

"Thank you," I said, smiling falsely, because my own desire with Mr. Harte and Cinnamon Ridge was never to see either again. We peeled Annie away (she had discovered that one cop had five children and she was bent on getting them all to Toybrary next Thursday) and got into the van. Price, of course, took out his hostilities by going around corners too fast—this while a police car was yards behind us. I was tossed across the backseat into Michael because I was slow getting my seatbelt latched. Michael caught me and held me next to him. The warmth of his body seeped through his clothing and mine and left me hot and gasping.

"So how's that check made out, Fraser?" said Price.

I looked. "To me."

Price howled with delight. "We sure earned it, getting hassled like that. I hate cops. Let's go cash the check."

I could not believe he had said that.

"Oh, Price," said Annie, laughing more than frowning. Annie, who teaches Sunday school and is as morally upright as anyone I know. "Stop your nonsense. It's for Toybrary."

"Okay," said Price meekly.

Price.

Meek.

It was only slightly less amazing than that Annie had addressed him as if she were his mother. Tough wild Price, meek as an automatic shift for Annie. Musical sweet Annie, a stern parent to Price.

"Well, let's pool the money we're allowed to use," said Price, giving Annie a mock glare, "and go for pizza."

That means we won't get home for another two hours, I thought. And I have so much homework. Chemistry, botany, an English essay, those history chapters to read—

Ordinarily I do my homework Friday afternoon to get it over with. But Friday afternoon Michael and I had gone with Price and Annie to a basketball game; Friday evening the movies; Saturday all four of us up to the lake to see if the ice was hard enough for skating. (It wasn't.)

And Sunday mornings I work. My only revenue is seven hours delivering for a florist—churches, homes and hospitals. I like the job partly because of the money and partly because everybody is glad to get flowers. I had rushed home from my last delivery, choked down a peanut-butter sandwich (I don't even like peanut butter; its only advantage is that it's quick) and rushed over to Annie's so we could go get Mr. Harte's log cabin.

I was very tired. And very nervous about the amount of studying still ahead. "Maybe we'd better skip pizza today," I said. "I have an awful lot of homework."

49

I waited for Annie to back me up. We always support each other, and anyway, she would know I had said that partly for her. Annie has reserved Sunday afternoons for extra violin practice ever since I first met her. But Annie said, irritably, "Oh, Fraser. Come on. You get straight A's. It won't kill you to skip a night of studying."

I don't get straight A's. There have been semesters when I didn't even get straight B's. But I give off an aura of academic success that even Annie believes in.

It was so strange to be sitting in that van, the darkness of winter afternoons closing in on us, and know that my best friend was in the front seat—and she was not my ally. Annie's voice had tightened in annoyance at *me*. Here was Price wanting to rip off Toybrary and she had just laughed! And what about her violin? Her days were certainly as busy as mine; she hadn't fit in any practice Friday or Saturday. Her lesson was still coming up Monday.

"I want mozzarella and pepperoni," said Annie. "But if you want it all the way, Price, I can just pick the onions and peppers and stuff off mine and give them to you."

They argued about pizza toppings.

Michael said softly, "Fraser?"

"What?"

"What have you got in your boots? Fire?"

I glanced down. My cords had worked out of my boots. Peeking above the leather were my gaudy flame-patterned knee socks.

"Oh," said Michael. "Socks." He pulled the hem of my trousers up higher. His fingers whispered along the nubble of the knitting and I nearly climbed up him. We looked at each other instead of at my socks, and I forgot log cabins and homework and even Annie.

Chapter 5

By Christmas, Michael and I and Annie and Price were linked in everything we did. If I got a party invitation, the hostess added, "And of course you'll be bringing Michael." If Michael learned about anything interesting to do, we both went. If Price was in the mood for something different, he consulted Annie first, and then Michael and me, and we all went. Or we all didn't go.

I memorized Michael's phone number. I knew his favorite expressions, the topping he preferred on his ice-cream sundaes, and the trick he had of closing his eyes just before he answered an important question. I knew the taste of his lips, the texture of his hair and the feel of my hand in his.

We found our spot in school. Next to Annie's double-wide locker by the music room, where she keeps her violin. The boys found ways to meet us there—before school, between classes, after school.

My parents met Michael and pronounced him wonderful. "Oh, Fraser," said my mother after Michael had dinner with us one night. "How lucky you are to have a boy who can be such a good friend. Your father and I are like that."

She gave me a long hug and then pushed me away from her, still holding me, and she looked at me approvingly for several seconds. "I'm so happy for you. You'll be one of these women who has it all. I can tell. Fine career. Fine husband. Fine—"

"Slow down," said my father. "She's only seventeen. I haven't even taken her on weekend college campus hunts yet. Let's not marry her off please."

Ben and Lynn met Michael a few days later. Afterward Lynn said I was unbelievably lucky. She had had to wait until she was twenty to meet a gem like that. Ben pretended to glare at her. "You didn't meet me till you were twenty-one," he said.

"Ah, but I was daydreaming about you when I was twenty," said Lynn, and they laughed and kissed.

Study time dwindled almost to nothing. Somehow I crammed my math assignments in between toy loans and prepared for quizzes while I set my hair.

And so my life filled with Michael, as a soda glass fills with froth, and everything that was not Michael floated away.

"Fraser," said Annie. We were talking on the phone, of course. It was the only way we ever communicated now—by wire. It subtracted a dimension from our friendship. We did not talk face to face. It's as if she's already gone to college, I thought. We're too lazy to write letters, so we call each other up.

"What?" I said. I was doodling. For weeks I had doodled variations of Michael's name. Now I was drawing little birds—fat cozy birds with their wings tucked in tight. I circled the rectangular phone pad with a flock of identical birds.

"I'm switching my English class. I convinced the guidance counselor I need my music sessions back to back, and that meant I could only squeeze English in fifth period, and the only class small enough to accept another student is Price's. Isn't that clever?"

"No," I said. "You have enough trouble paying attention to English under the best of circumstances. Now you won't be paying attention to anything but Price."

"You're wrong, Fraser. I work better with Price around. Either I'm showing off for him, or he has a soothing effect."

It had to be the first, because Price was the least soothing person I knew.

"You could change your American History class," Annie suggested. "Then you could be with Michael more. Don't you miss him a lot during the day?"

But I did not miss him during the day. Sometimes I felt as if the only thing I did was spend time with Michael. What had happened to the rest of my life? I dashed through things like botany lab, I postponed things like my ophthalmologist appointment. I never saw Connie or Susannah or Smedes or Julie except in gym. I never went for solitary walks. I never read a book. I was learning how to ski. I was learning how to program a microcomputer. I was eating fewer hamburgers and more pizza, because Price and Michael both loved pizza so much. I was spending every cent I earned from delivering flowers on my share of the dates.

And yet, every time I saw Michael I was so overwhelmingly glad to see him that I couldn't seem to care about my scheduling problems or the things I wasn't doing. They receded, like a tide, and became too distant to care much about.

But Annie didn't wait for my answer. She had another topic. "Price and I are going to a professional ice-hockey game this weekened. He can get two more tickets. You and Michael want to come?"

My pen made a big splotchy scratch across the last little bird. "Ice hockey?" I repeated. "But Annie! You hate violence." Annie wouldn't watch a television show unless somebody assured her that it contained zero violence. She couldn't even sit in the cafeteria if there were loud arguments going on. And after one junior-high soccer game, when the teams began beating up on each other and the referees and parents were pulling them away, bleeding and missing teeth, she refused ever to see another soccer game.

"Annie, if you won't go see soccer games," I said, "which are very innocent gentle games in comparison to ice hockey—"

"I know, I know. But Price likes ice hockey. And I like to do the things he does."

"Oh, Annie!" I cried, and I stood up holding the telephone as if it were an instrument of violence itself— as if my own thoughts were going to electrocute me. "Do you ever think we shouldn't be doing this?"

"Doing what?"

"I don't really know. Do you ever feel threatened by all this? Do you ever think it's wrong?"

Annie's side of the phone was silent. Annie is never silent. Finally she said, "Don't you feel well, Fraser?"

I thought about that. I even looked down at myself and I knew I was fine. No ear infections. No fever. "No, I don't," I said to her. I stumbled for words. "It's—it's—Annie, we're going too far."

"*Oh, Fray!*" There was shock and fascination in her voice. "Oh, no! What have you and Michael been *doing*? And I thought Price and I were going pretty far. Oh, God, Fray. Maybe you should call that number in the classifieds for birth-control information."

"Annie, I'm not talking about sex," I cried. "Sex has nothing to do with it."

"It doesn't?" said Annie. "Then what are you talking about. You said you went too far."

"I didn't mean sex, Annie. I meant—" But she had annoyed me and I had lost the thought. I no longer knew what I had meant, or even what the subject had been. I felt silly standing up at attention next to the telephone.

"I thought you were going to tell me what it's like to lose your virginity," said Annie. "Now, that would have been interesting. But anything else would be boring after all those expectations. Now, are you coming to the ice-hockey game or not?"

Michael leaned over and whispered in my ear, "I can't believe how bored I am. I've memorized the patron list."

Price, on my right, murmured even more softly,

"Not as bored as I am, Michael. I've penciled in all the o's on the program."

"What piece are we on now?" Michael breathed in my ear.

I tapped the program.

"Which movement?" he said.

"Third. Two after this."

Michael and Price were slumped down on the velveteen auditorium seats, their long legs stretched out under the seats in front of them, threatening the ankles of the viewers there. Michael's hands were jammed in his pockets, a very awkward maneuver, given the angle of his legs.

Michael, frantic for something to do, began leafing through the photographs in my wallet. Between movements of the string concerto, he whispered to Price, "I am now intimately acquainted with Fraser's nephew Jake at age four weeks, eight weeks and twelve weeks."

"Let me see those next," said Price.

We had brought them to Annie's chamber concert. After all, Annie had gone to their ice hockey, and I was learning their cross-country skiing. Usually I like snow. It's pretty and white and makes me feel all sorts of Christmasy emotions, like hope and love and charity. Now I was extremely grateful that all snows so far this winter had been paltry and had quickly melted.

We should have started them on something easy to listen to, I thought. A pops concert, say. But not Bartok. Not Webern.

"Music sounds mutilated," muttered Price.

"Let's stick to ice hockey," said Michael.

"Be quiet," I said, before the lady in front of me did. I thought, if they tell Annie how bored they are, when she's been practicing so many months for this concert, I'll kill them.

But I had underestimated them. They were so glad when the concert finally ended they jumped to their feet and participated loudly in the standing ovation. "I didn't think you liked it that much," I said to Michael.

"I hated it," he said cheerfully. "I never want to do this again. I cannot believe you've suffered through this kind of thing before and actually willingly agreed to repeat it."

"Then why are you clapping so much?" I said.

"Because it's over," said Price, and the boys laughed. "Don't worry," said Price. "We won't tell Annie anything except how terrific she looked. How many more concerts does she have?"

The rest of her life, I thought. "Several each year."

"None that I'm attending," said Michael.

Annie emerged, carrying her violin in its case. She was wearing a silvery-white blouse with a black velvet ribbon, and a black satiny concert skirt. Her cheeks were flushed with pride and she was absolutely beautiful. "What a concert!" she said. "Wasn't it wonderful, Price?"

"Yes," said Price immediately, bending over and kissing her. "Absolutely wonderful. You are fantastic. Let's go celebrate. How about Le Fine Bouche for dessert?"

"Phone call for you, Fraser," said Miss Herschel, peering around the corner, her hair in her eyes. I longed to take scissors and remove the offending hair.

I took the call at her children's book desk. It was

Annie. "I wondered where you were," I said. "Are you coming to Toybrary late?"

"Oh, Fray, forgive me. Promise you'll forgive me?"

I knew that voice. That was the voice she used with all her old friends who wrote to her and she never wrote back to. They'd telephone after six months to find out if she was dead. "For what?" I said.

"I can't come. I have to practice the violin. We have that big dress rehearsal coming up with the visiting string quartet and now Price wants me to go with him this afternoon to look at racing bicycles. He's decided it's never going to snow this year and we should take up another sport. Oh, Fraser, it's so hard to practice now. Price can't stand the music I'm doing."

"Racing bicycles?" I repeated. It was beyond imagination, putting Annie on a racing bike.

"The things we do for them," Annie agreed morosely. "Oh, well. Anyway, I can't make Toybrary. Can you carry it alone today?"

"I guess so. It's pretty slow."

Annie hung up so fast I still had the phone to my ear. There is no sound on earth more empty, more alien, than the buzz of a disconnected telephone. If snow makes me feel hopeful and loving, an empty phone makes me feel alien and abandoned. I set my phone down quickly.

"Hullo, Fraser!" cried Kit Lipton, bouncing into Toybrary and hugging me enthusiastically. "Guess what I want this time!"

I grinned at her. "Let's see. This pretty new doll-house furniture we just got in? See the tiny blue wing chair? It's even got two tiny-teeny pillows and an *eensy* lace decoration for the back of the chair."

"It's called an antimacassar," Kit told me. "I know, because my grandmother inherited some from her grandmother. No. I have something to tell you, Fraser."

"What's that, Kit?"

"I've outgrown dolls."

She stood there so seriously. I wanted to hug her eleven times and tell her she was my favorite little girl in the whole world. That she could play with dolls all her life as far as I was concerned, and grow up to design them, too.

"I'm going to be a scientist, like you," she informed me.

"Like me? I'm not a scientist," I protested.

"Yes, you are. Your photograph was in the paper last week. My mother showed me. You and seven other people at the high school are taking your science projects to the state science fair. I'm going to be a scientist too, so give me a science thing to check out."

I nearly wept. I'm so emotional today, I thought. I wonder if it's true about premenstrual syndrome. "Well, let's see. We haven't much in right now. A microscope kit. A Sun Graphics kit. A project pamphlet on snow crystals and a metal detector."

"What do you recommend?" said Kit. Her eyes were fixed on me as if I were God, about to redistribute brains and ability.

"Sun Graphics. You'll make prints of leaves using sunlight and shadow."

"It's winter," she objected. "There are no leaves."

"Nobody said it would be easy being a scientist," I told her, and she left laughing.

Two little boys exchanged video-game cartridges. An adult checked out Pente. A girl about twelve returned a detective kit that claimed to offer hours of fun and excitement. "It's boring," she said accusingly. "Boring, *boring, boring.* You shouldn't have given it to me. I planned my whole weekend around it and I was *bored.* It wasn't even interesting for five *minutes.*"

"Then how come it's a week overdue?" I snapped. The nerve of these kids, I thought. I kill myself laying in these toys and I'm *still* responsible. They have a boring weekend and it's my fault. "What do you want? A money-back guarantee?"

Naturally she left without checking out another toy, and Miss Herschel could not get her to take a book either. "Great work, Fraser," called Miss Herschel. "Alienate a few more people, will you?"

"Sure," I said.

Boredom and anger and pressure crawled over me like bugs. The Science Fair project isn't ready, I thought. And I'm the one who's behind, not the other girls. And we have that extra Madrigals Choir rehearsal coming up. And I have no doubt whatsoever that on Wednesday next week Mr. McGrath is going to assign the term papers. How am I supposed to see Michael with all this junk cluttering up my life?

I sat down and color-coded the play money in a newly returned Monopoly set. I was tempted to look up who had borrowed it, telephone them, and scream at them for not returning it in good condition, but I restrained myself. A terrible thought slithered into my mind, taking my words and inverting them.

How am I supposed to lead my life, with Michael cluttering it up?

I caught the thought and killed it, superstitiously, as if I could actually stomp it out, like a brush fire. And looked up to see wispy blond hair. Thin shy face. "Hello, Katurah," I said.

Michael's here. Something in me bent, and relaxed, and I sagged mentally the way I did physically—slumping with relief. All these crazy thoughts will vanish now. Michael's here. The moment I see him I won't feel this way.

"Look at my Christmas doll," said Katurah. "She's why I haven't come in lately. I've been playing with her all the time, and she came with lots and lots of clothes."

A Victorian doll. The kind that the woman who built Annie's mansion must have given her children. Large, beautiful, graceful, dressed in lace and velvet, with china hands and lovely leather-buttoned boots. A doll to sit on a window seat in a turret, and dream of gazebos and roses.

"I named her Viola Maude," said Katurah. "Just like you told me."

"I love her," I told Katurah. "She's a perfect Viola Maude."

"But now I'm bored with her," said Katurah. "Now I want to check out Chinese Checkers or else Leverage."

"They both take two players," I warned her. All these bored kids, I thought. It's boring to have them tell me they're bored. I am so sick of Toybrary. I have to find someone else to do this for me. If I'm not going to have Annie to share these hours with, forget it.

"Michael will play with me," said Katurah with absolute certainty.

"Oh, yeah?" said Michael, looming over us. I looked up the wide wales of his corduroy trousers, past his pullover sweater, into his laughing brown eyes and I

61

loved him. He is perfect, I thought. I'm the one who's crazy. Imagining there's something wrong.

"Yeah," said Katurah, in the voice of a gangster who will otherwise put cement on your ankles and drown you. Michael laughed. With his left hand he pulled her hair; with his right hand he found the nape of my neck and stroked it.

Miss Herschel agreed to watch Toybrary while I took a break. We drove to a Dairy Queen. I ate a chocolate sundae and gave Katurah my maraschino cherry. Michael told me about a computer program he was writing to keep track of his father's philately.

"That's stamps," said Katurah. "My stepfather loves stamps." Clearly people who loved stamps were to be suspected of other sinister things too. "In fact, that's why Michael is baby-sitting me tonight. They've gone to a big stamp show."

"How interesting," I said, although it was not, and I fervently hoped Michael did not expect me to take up stamps. "Does Judith like stamps, too? Is that how they met?"

"No, that's Dad's consuming passion," said Michael. "Judith took it up when they got married. Judith used to go to Audubon Society. She was always going off on owl prowls at four in the morning."

"Owl prowls! Now that sounds exciting." I was definitely going to be on Judith's team now.

"It's not," Katurah informed me. "It's cold and dark and all the owls do is hoot and fly away."

"Now if only we could figure out a way to get *you* to hoot and fly away," Michael teased Katurah.

But she did not laugh. She took him literally. Her face grew pale and pinched and after a moment she stared back into the remains of her ice cream and shivered. "I'm sorry," said Michael swiftly, and he scooped her up in his lap and kissed her hair. "Here. Want some of my Coke? Want to play tic-tac-toe with me on the napkin? Nobody's going to run out on you again, Katurah."

I loved him even more. He could have ignored this new person in his life, this little girl who demanded a lot. But he had chosen to be her ally.

"Guess I'd better get you back to Toybrary," said Michael, reluctantly, and his eyes, dipping down toward Katurah, told me he needed to talk to her a little alone.

We went outside into softly falling snow.

"Snow!" cried Michael, and he laughed exuberantly, and hugged both of us. "I thought we'd never get snow! All Christmas vacation without a half an inch; all January without anything but ice. Snow! Thank God."

"I hate snow," said Katurah. "It's cold."

"We can cross-country ski Saturday," said Michael excitedly. "There are terrific trails up at Spring Meadow. Fraser, don't forget to go to Action Sports and rent your equipment tomorrow. They might be out if you wait till Saturday morning."

"Spring Meadow is a dumb name for a snow place," observed Katurah. "Ugh. Michael, don't kiss her. I hate kissing."

"And then afterward, we can go down to my basement," added Michael, ignoring Katurah and kissing me again. "I've got a new computer game. You'll love it."

"Michael, I've told you and told you. I don't love computer games. They're always war. You have to kill to survive. I don't like being pitted against you like that. Anyway, on Saturday I was going to go shopping with my mother."

"You can shop any time," said Michael. "Don't forget to rent the skis. Here we are. Say Hi to Toybrary for me." He leaned over both of us to open the passenger door for me, and kissed me as he did so. Katurah, between us, said, "You're smothering me, Michael."

"All in a good cause," said Michael.

I love you, I thought. I love your lips and your hair. I love how nice you are to Katurah and to me. I have to learn to love the things you enjoy, too. Look on the bright side. It could be stamps.

Chapter 6

I did not start Toybrary on purpose.

It began of its own accord because I happened to speak out of turn in front of Miss Herschel. I was not at the library by choice. There was a term-paper assignment, and I was bored, because it was a contemporary subject. I detest newspaper files, microfiche and microfilm. I just like books. Facts are so much more factual in books.

The topic was war. We had to list every single war now occurring on the globe and analyze its current status. I had had no idea how many people were working at killing one another off. Africa, the Near East, the Middle East, the Far East, islands in this ocean, islands in that ocean, all of Central America . . .

Needless to say, I tired of all this bloodshed. I began circling the library looking for something to break the monotony of brother gunning down brother. Actually, I was hoping to find a handsome youth with blond hair and broad shoulders who would be so struck by my brains and beauty that he'd carry me off into the sunset. Or at least as far as McDonald's. But I didn't know most of the boys at the library the day Toybrary was born. It's harder than you think to strike up a conversation in a library. Heads are bent over books. Faces are hidden by periodical indexes. Hands are closed around pencils, not other hands. Everybody has postponed his research till the last possible moment, and who has time for romance when there are six more sources to investigate?

The only boy doing nothing had pimples and sagging socks and wasn't fourteen if he was a day, so I ended up talking to the children's librarian.

"What we need, Fraser," said Miss Herschel, "is something that will really bring people in."

I thought the library was jammed and the atmosphere would have been much more pleasant with *fewer* people, but perhaps I was just naturally antisocial after all this war reading. "Maybe if you offered something besides books," I suggested.

I wasn't thinking about anything. I wasn't even thinking. I was just there, propped up by Miss Herschel's desk, killing time.

"Something besides books?" she repeated.

"I read about a library in New Hampshire that also loans toys. They have everything. Especially stuff that people would love to have but don't buy because they might not use it more than once. Giant stuffed giraffes or unusual board games. And standard stuff—wooden blocks, Teddy bears, Monopoly."

"Fraser! What a wonderful idea!" she cried. "Look into this at once. Set aside war temporarily. Look up toy-lending libraries and see how they did it."

We peacemongers are all happy to set aside war temporarily, so I dipped into the newspaper indexes to find out about toy lending.

It *was* a better topic than war—but only marginally. Because somehow, between the looking-up and the talking-about and the expanding-upon, old Fraser MacKendrick became the chief administrative officer of Toybrary.

I gave a speech to the P.T.A. and didn't die of fear and didn't forget any of the words, and in fact the Junior Women's Club asked me to talk to them too. I learned how to address groups, and how not to be afraid of an audience and how to convince them to donate to my cause. My father said, "Fraser, if you never learn any other skill in your entire life, you will get good jobs, because you'll be able to get money out of sticky club fingers."

Toybrary was an astonishing success. Organizing Toybrary, establishing it, advertising it were as much fun as I had ever had in my life. But from there on in, it was down hill.

Miss Herschel was too busy to administer it. Annie surrendered to my appeals and helped, and then she convinced Susannah to pitch in too. Susannah was a help in a dim-witted sort of way, and the three of us operated Toybrary from three till eight, in overlapping shifts.

With appalling speed, Toybrary became just another dull routine in my week.

It was a bad season for local news (no wars in

Chapman), and we were pounced upon by television, radio and newspaper. After you have been on morning talk shows, giving examples of the fine things our youth can accomplish, expounding on your imagination, community spirit and hard work, it's embarrassing to say the following week, "Actually this is boring and I quit."

Nevertheless that's just what Susannah did. She began dating Matt, and although Matt would never be number one on my list—or even number fifty—he was certainly more interesting than a Barbie Doll swimming-pool set.

I stayed with Toybrary but I would wish that I was still just starting it; that was fun. Launching anything was always so much more interesting than actually doing it.

Then I'd wish that I had never gotten into Toybrary at all, that I had met some fantastic eighteen-year-old with brains, manners, a sense of humor, looks, build and a classic Corvette . . .

I sat at the Toybrary desk, my knees hunched near my chin, checking to be sure there were still dice in the Parcheesi game, and I thought, Five out of six isn't bad. I have to relax about Michael. I'm not some rigid type whose life can't expand to include new things. What kind of relationship am I going to have with him if I keep complaining and whining whenever he suggests something?

"Dropping out of Madrigals?" said Mrs. Ierardi. Her long thin face became longer and thinner. She regarded me as the Revolutionary troops must have looked at Benedict Arnold. "But Fraser, we need you. You're the best low alto we've got."

Ordinarily I love compliments. This one upset me. "Really, it's a good time for this," I said. "We've finished the winter concerts, and it's another five weeks before the spring concerts. Lots of time to audition more altos."

Mrs. Ierardi frowned at me. "Fraser, you of all people need to stay in Madrigals. You lead a very intellectual life. Singing is one of the outlets you need."

"I took up skiing, you know. And—and other things. I just don't have time for Madrigals any more. I'm sorry, Mrs. Ierardi. I'll miss it a lot. But I have to drop out."

And Michael could not stand classical music. He refused to go to any more of Annie's concerts. He had not even managed to sit still through a tape of my last Madrigal concert. And he was free the two afternoons Madrigals practiced.

"I understand you have quite a firm relationship with the Hollander boy," said Mrs. Ierardi.

It was like having someone dip into my head without permission. Gossip, I thought. Thin beady-eyed old gossip.

"Don't lose your head over him," said Mrs. Ierardi.

"I am not losing my head," I said, trying not to yell. "That sounds like some wimpy little cheerleader going haywire because some boy smiles at her."

"Well?" said Mrs. Ierardi.

I could have kicked her. *"Well?"* As if Mrs. Ierardi, and all her gossipy teacher cronies, had decided that Fraser MacKendrick had "lost her head over the Hollander boy."

"I'm too busy for Madrigals, Mrs. Ierardi," I said.

"He ought to be able to give up a little for you," she

snapped. "This is not nineteen fifty-five. You don't have to rebuild your life to suit the whims of some boy."

"I am not following Michael's whims. We're *both* giving up a lot. He's quitting Computer Club. And he was going to teach a class in game design, too. And I'm quitting Madrigals. We have to have the time."

"And what are you going to do with that time?" demanded Mrs. Ierardi, as if it were her business. "Go sit at the Dairy Queen and have a sundae together? Kiss on the couch? You can do that any time. Don't surrender what counts, Fraser."

"I'm just officially telling you I am no longer a member of the Madrigal Choir," I said stiffly, and I walked out of the room, and I was shaking all over.

"You wouldn't believe how she talked to me," I told Michael. We were not at the Dairy Queen. We would have been, but I felt self-conscious about choosing it after what Mrs. Ierardi had said. We were at McDonald's instead, having cheeseburgers, although I was in a chocolate-marshmallow-sundae mood. When you are angry, a cheeseburger is gone in three furious chomps. You need soft ice cream to slide gently down, wrapped in chocolate, to soothe your distressed throat.

"I would believe," said Michael. "Mr. Duffy really threw it at me. He says anyone with a grain of responsibility wouldn't do this to him. I pointed out that Dick Biaggio agreed to take the class for me, and Dick knows how to write game programs as well as I do, but Mr. Duffy said that didn't matter. I was the one who agreed to teach the class and I was the one who drew up the curriculum and I was the one the kids signed up to study with and therefore I was the one who should be ashamed of myself. Putting my own selfish desires ahead of my commitments."

"Sometimes I think they become teachers just so they can impose their beliefs on other people," I said.

"Like my father," agreed Michael, chewing on French fries and angrily grinding his teeth. "He's harping on college now. I'm a junior, I don't have to apply till next fall, but he says we have to visit at least a dozen colleges before I can possibly make a judgment on where to apply. Every weekend he wants to do this, Fraser. I mean, when would we get together?"

Visiting colleges! I could see broad grassy campuses—well, snowy, at this time of year, anyhow—dormitories, brick buildings, huge libraries, hundreds of college students rushing from class to class. Visiting a dozen of them. "That sounds like such fun, though," I said. "I won't get to do that. I'll be going to State. My whole family went to State, and anyway, it's all we can afford." The only activity my mother was still active in was the Alumni Association. Of course, I reflected, Dad was active in it too; probably she'd drop out of even that if he weren't involved.

"I don't want to do it," said Michael definitively. "I want to be with you."

I felt the way Katurah had felt when Michael leaned over her to kiss me. *You're suffocating me*, I thought. But that can't be. This is the way it works. My mother and father. Ben and Lynn. Price and Annie. Matt and Susannah. Even Mr. Hollander and Judith.

But Mr. Duffy doesn't think so. Mrs. Ierardi doesn't think so. So who's right? How do you do this, anyway? How far do you go? Forget sex. Sex is a pretty simple decision. Either you do it or you don't. But sharing. How much do you share?

We tossed our hamburger wrappers into the trash and walked out to Judith's car. It was very cold, but when Michael opened the door for me, I slipped into a greenhouse of heat from the sun shining through the windshield.

Don't think about it, I told myself.

"Kiss me," said Michael, and I kissed him, and it was easy to think of nothing but that.

Annie was sitting in her bedroom window seat, framed between the gray of the sky and the cream of the walls. I was flopped on her bed.

Thank God for friendship, I thought. How terrible if our friendship had foundered on jealousy. If what was between Annie and me turned out to be a fad, like racketball or needlepoint, each a short season of pleasure and then rapid boredom. Because now I really do have something to talk about. Something I can't express to Michael or my mother or anyone but Annie. No one but Annie could understand.

I said, "What's the definition of a perfect couple, Annie?"

I've missed girls, I thought. You can go on being honest with them. But there's something about a boy friend. The more your lives entwine, the harder it is to be honest. The more tangled you get, the more complex your thoughts get. Is it because there's more room for hurt than with a girl?

"That's easy," said Annie. "Price and I are a perfect couple. You and Michael. Look at these maroon legwarmers Price gave me for Christmas. I hate maroon. I don't have a single thing to go with maroon. I have to buy a whole new outfit just to put Price's legwarmers on."

I lay down on her bed, with its old ragged cotton bedspread, and stared up at the ceiling. "Annie, do you ever feel—oh, I don't know—do you ever feel—"

"Why, Fraser MacKendrick, English virtuoso, at a loss for words! But to answer your indirect question, yes. I always feel these days. I feel Price's lips, hands, hair, chest—"

"I don't mean that, Annie. I'm serious. Really serious. I meant, is this what you had in mind? All those years we daydreamed?"

"Absolutely. It's perfect. All I have to do is coach Price in color combinations." Her voice was warm, like the low notes on her violin. "The first time we kissed," Annie told me, "I felt my entire life shift. Like an instrument changing keys."

"But did you want it to shift that much?" I sat up. Annie sleeps in a flock of pillows. I gathered several of them in my arms, and spoke while I hugged them to me. "Annie, sometimes I don't even want to hear Michael's voice on the telephone."

"How strange," said Annie. "Does Michael have some dreadful flaw in his character that I haven't noticed?"

"No, no. He's wonderful. I think it's me." I was desperate for Annie to understand. But she seemed so blank to me—so removed. As if Price counted, but her best friend, Fraser, that girl she used to play with on the back steps, was someone she only vaguely remembered.

"What about you? Your teeth are straight. Your figure is a model's dream. Your hair is satin honey."

"Not my body, Annie. Not Michael's body either. I just sometimes feel overpowered."

Annie laughed. "I love it. The cover of adult romances. Where the masterful man stands behind the delicate shoulder of the helpless girl and you can't decide if he's going to lead her astray or guide her into happiness ever after."

There is nothing worse than trying to express a profound thought and having the other person not catch on. You feel stupid, and you feel angry, and what's worse, you really do feel helpless. Words aren't going to get you anywhere. "I'm not helpless, Annie. You don't understand. It just doesn't feel one hundred per cent right to me. I have all these doubts about it— about me, about Michael and me."

"Oh, Fraser," said Annie, and the irritation surfaced in her voice instead of mine. "There's no such thing as one hundred per cent right. The finest musical performance in the world could still be improved. The best paper ever written could still include more information. Michael is as close to perfection as boys come. You should be thrilled. It's so annoying to have you get so picky every time we turn around. What in the world is there for you to be discontented about?"

I got off the bed. Annie has two full-length mirrors, so she can see herself from any angle. I caught my expression in them. I looked fretful. Whining. Like the little kids at Toybrary when their mothers won't let them take out toys with 498 pieces.

"Your complexion is perfect," said Annie. "Stop worrying."

"It's not my complexion, Annie. It's life."

"Believe me, Fraser, this life beats the one where we hung around a gazebo exchanging watermelons and pretended that life was splendid without boys."

She began talking about Price, about their plans for the future, about college and marriage.

I felt like a child Kit Lipton's age. Still bogged down in roller skates, ballerina costumes, Barbie Dolls and bubble bath. It was Annie who had crossed the line into adulthood: into that pairing-off that everybody, from my mother to Lynn to Judith, strived for. I was still a child.

I looked around Annie's room and saw that many of the watermelons had made way for photographs of Price, for dinner menus where she had eaten with Price, for a faded corsage Price had given her.

We really are just watermelon friends now, I thought. Friends left over from grade school. Friends who skinned their knees together and learned jump-rope rhymes together and practiced putting on mascara together back when they still weren't allowed to wear makeup out of the house.

I'm the one who's immature, I thought. All this time I prided myself on being mature. I was the organizer. The one who gave speeches and mustered group efforts and rallied people to work with me. Annie was the simple-minded violinist who tagged along.

I had it backward. Annie's the adult. Look at her with Price. I can't share that much. My whole life? Are they kidding? They really want me to take my entire life and fold it into Michael's like one strand of a braid?

I'm like a spill, I thought. Michael is like a paper towel.

If I lie down next to him, I'll be absorbed, until I'm nothing but Michael. Except that Michael is perfect. I've never known a boy as wonderful.

"Oh, that reminds me," said Annie, but I had not been listening, and I did not know what reminded her of something. "I stumbled on a Christmas present I made for you and forgot to give you. Oh, well. You can save it for next year."

She handed me a tiny tree ornament. It was circular gold with a scrap of cross-stitch in it. I hoped she had dated it, because my watermelon collection was so extensive I tended to forget what arrived when. "Why, thanks, Annie," I said, "another wa—"

But it was not a watermelon.

In deep electric-blue, tiny delicate crosses said

MICHAEL AND FRASER

I ran my fingers around the frame. Round, unending, in wedding-ring gold. I shivered. "You did a lovely job," I told her.

But the shiver persisted.

Chapter 7

"Term papers!" trilled Mr. McGrath musically.

All teachers have mannerisms. Sometimes you last all year without being irritated; sometimes the irritation sets in September fourth. Mr. McGrath's habit of singing our assignments had been irking me since about Thanksgiving. "Term papers!" he caroled again, more to himself than to us, as if there was some deep delight in term papers that we could not understand. He's caroled "Term papers!" every February for fifteen years, I thought, and he'll go on caroling it every February for twenty more. I don't think I want to be a teacher. I want to do something more exciting than assign term papers to hapless students.

"We have here," cried Mr. McGrath, like a priest

learning chant, "a list of seventy-five obscure Americans. You will have to do research in order to know which of them you want to research, as you will have heard of none of them. But each, in his or her own special way, contributed something meaningful to the culture, to the inheritance, to the very space that we citizens occupy today."

"Ugh," said the class in unison.

I looked at the list and was thankful that my science project was wrapped up. Blue-green algae were not destined to be a lifelong passion for me. We returned from the Science Fair prizeless; there were countless exhibits far more original than ours. I had spent most of the weekend tense, because there was a school dance that Michael wanted to go to; and, of course, we missed it.

The names were in alphabetical order, but other than that there were no clues. I knew I would do a woman, and I read through the names to find women. Even in obscurity, women seemed to do less than men when it came to American history. Only nine of the names were women. If I don't choose one right now, it'll get taken, I thought.

I stared hard at the names, trying to guess by their shape and symmetry which belonged to someone interesting. Annie and I were always attracted by special names. We used to love naming the litters of kittens her mama cat had. I remember one litter of all black kittens we named Rainbow, Crayon, Iris and Daffodil because they weren't. "I'll do Eliza Lucas Pinckney," I announced.

Mr. McGrath checked her off. She was mine. I looked at her name again and began to feel a strange excitement percolating in me. I didn't know whether Eliza was an early doctor or a pioneer Congresswoman, whether she had done this in Maine or Oregon, and if it was in 1840 or 1910. I'll start on Eliza this Saturday, I thought. I'll drive to the State University Library to research her.

"The paper will be no more than thirty pages long and no less than twenty," said Mr. McGrath. "You will use no fewer than ten sources and some of them must be periodicals. The bibliography must be correctly compiled according to the rule book you have from sophomore year. Two points will be deducted for each spelling error. Anyone using an encyclopedia in his bibliography will lose one grade."

The classroom was like a chorus, with Mr. McGrath uttering his guidelines and the kids moaning after each one. Little cries of "That's too much, Mr. McGrath" and "But I'm on the baseball team and I don't have time for all this" filled the room. Mr. McGrath simply went on caroling, "Term papers!"

I told Michael about it when we met by Annie's locker between fourth and fifth period. "I love research," I said. "It's so exciting. You find a sentence here and a clue there and you piece this person together. It's like a treasure hunt."

Michael stared at me as if I were insane. "I hate research," he said emphatically. "I like it all prepared for me, ready to read."

"I was thinking I'd get started Saturday. Look Eliza up at the State University Library for a few hours."

"But Fraser," protested Michael, "we were going skiing on Saturday. You can research Eliza any time. Besides, you don't even know who she is yet. Maybe there's a biography on her at the local library in Chapman."

"I like big libraries. Sitting with all the college kids. Walking past a million books. Anyhow, we've been skiing four straight weekends in a row, and it should be clear to you that skiing is not my strong point. You go skiing. I'll go to the library."

Michael sighed. "All right. If you can wait to get started until after lunch, I'll drive you up."

"No, no. You ski. I'll research alone."

"Come on, Fray. We just got out of Computer Club and Madrigals in order to spend time together, and you're arranging to spend an entire Saturday without me? Be kind. You're kind to animals. Be kind to me."

During a slow period at Toybrary, I crossed the library to look Eliza up in the *Dictionary of American Biography*.

Pilsbury . . . Pinchback . . . Pinckney, Charles . . . Pinckney, Charles Cotesworth . . . Pinckney, Eliza Lucas (1722–1793).

Oh, good, I thought. Colonial and Revolutionary War. I like that period.

Eliza turned out to be some woman. At age sixteen she managed three plantations in South Carolina—by herself. She set out live oak trees for future navies. She studied enough law to draft wills for her poorer neighbors. Because her plantations were mortgaged, she had to find a profitable crop. She revived silk culture and directed experiments with flax and hemp. She was the first person in South Carolina to make a success of growing the dye indigo. She was also, said the *Dictionary*, "popular in Charleston society."

I lost interest in anything besides Eliza. She was my kind of person. I tried to imagine her—sixteen, seventeen, eighteen; dancing at the balls in Charleston by night, running agricultural experiments by day. What color is indigo? I thought.

I could feel her, across the years. Eliza. Even her name sounded strong.

I thought I was pretty terrific, running Toybrary. Big deal. I didn't introduce new crops to the New World.

"Fraser," interrupted Miss Herschel with extreme annoyance. I jumped. I had been in Colonial South Carolina with Eliza. "All these phone calls on the library line are unacceptable. You tell them to call you at home. Is that clear?"

"Yes, Miss Herschel," I said. I hate being yelled at. I can't help feeling that at my age I should be past that. Miss Herschel and I should have a conference if she doesn't like what I'm doing; she shouldn't yell at me as if I were nine. "I'm sorry," I said. "Who is it? I'll call him back."

"For once it isn't a him. It's a girl named Connie. She's still on the line."

"Connie! How neat. I haven't heard from her in ages."

"Don't use my phone to have your reunion," snapped Miss Herschel, and she stalked off to help a little boy find out about the longest, tallest, hugest and heaviest of all the things that fascinated him. About the only way to keep little boys from checking out war toys is to give them the *Guiness Book of Records*.

"Hi, Connie," I said happily. "How are you? Where've you been?"

"Where have *I* been?" said Connie. "*I've* been right here. *You*'re the one who's been away. In Michael's arms, presumably. A limited horizon, perhaps, but no doubt a satisfactory one."

I laughed. "It's great to hear from you."

Connie giggled. "You make it sound as if I've been out of the country for years. Try looking past Michael's shoulders once in a while. We're all still here. Listen, though. A few years ago your mother was interested in old bonnets and antique hats, and the Wickfield Museum is having an exhibit. Want to drive over Saturday with my mom and me?"

"Oh, Connie," I said. "Either I work on my term paper or I go skiing with Michael. I'd love to go with you, but I can't."

"Oh," said Connie politely. We went on talking for a few minutes, but there was nothing much to say. *I don't have time for you*, was the gist of my response. What a terrible thing for a friend to say, I thought. But I did not know how to retract it. It was true. I didn't have time for Connie.

Michael picked me up Saturday to drive to the University Library. I had my notebooks and pens. I like to take notes with a thin blue-tipped felt pen on narrow-lined white loose-leaf paper. If I don't use that paper and that pen, it doesn't feel as if I'm really taking notes.

Michael had borrowed Judith's car, a tiny old Datsun that was once white, but the Hollander clan, even the new members, are not of the car-washing habit, and now it was a speckled gray.

Above us the sky was a clear deep blue—a sky pretending to be July, but really icy, frigid, cruel February. So blue. I wondered what color Eliza's indigo had been—the same emotional, deep, piercing blue of the sky above me?

A thin white jet trail split the heavens. A stab of wanderlust cut me and I wanted to be on the plane, breaking sound barriers and going new places. "Michael," I said, "don't turn left, we have to get on the Interstate."

"We're not going to the library. There's something I want to show you on the computer," he said.

"Eliza predates computers. Come on, Michael, let's not waste time. I'm totally not in the mood for computers."

"Trust me," said Michael, and he was smiling a secret sort of smile, and I relented and let him drive on home. We went down to his sacred basement, me in a bad mood, because I wanted to look up at the blue sky and think about Eliza and indigo, and him in a terrific mood because of his computer secret.

We threaded among the video-game consoles, color television, radios, tape decks, light panel, and of course the modernistic desk that held the microcomputer, its screen and printer. I began to think longingly of Connie's trip to the museum to see all the old bonnets. Anything would be preferable to pretending interest in Michael's computer games.

Michael turned to me eagerly. Oh, God, he was so handsome. Tall and broad, and infinitely appealing when, as now, he was excited. "What I was thinking is this," he said, bursting with pleasure. "On your history project, we can file your notes on the disc. You won't have to bother with notebooks and messy papers. When it's time to write the final copy, we'll just call everything up on the screen. You can write here with me. The computer will print it out perfectly, and I have a spelling check program too, so you can't possibly make a spelling error."

I stared at him. This is my paper, I thought—about Eliza—the woman I picked. It has nothing to do with Michael.

"What do you think of these headings?" said Michael. "I put them in after you talked to me last night about Eliza." He jabbed a few buttons and called upon the screen his ideas for subdividing my paper. No fewer than twenty-three divisions had been provided for: food, dress, weather, climate, family, family history, health, indigo, silk, rice, plantation life, sons, education . . .

"Michael," I said, "it's a high-school paper, not a five-volume treatise on women in the Colonial South."

Michael paused and looked at me uncertainly.

"Anyhow, you can't seriously expect me to haul all my books from the library down here, type in the information when I don't even know how to type, and come to your house whenever I want to work on it. Really, Michael. It's far easier just to take pencil and paper to the library. Anyhow, it's my project and I'll do it my way."

His face closed in, white and pinched like Katurah's that day at the Dairy Bar, and he turned away from me.

From the day I began dating him, I had never hurt Michael. It was easy enough to do, that was clear. Just take all his efforts and throw them in his face as if they didn't matter. He didn't do all that for himself, I thought. He did it for me. What's the matter with me?

With a considerable effort Michael turned back, smiled at me ruefully, and said, "I guess you're right, Fray. I just got excited and didn't think. I'll drive you over to the library."

How I loved him. Using my nickname was like a verbal kiss across the room saying, I'm sorry, you're right, let's not fight. Fray. But I had no nicknames for Michael. He was not a Mike, not a Micky. I kissed him instead.

I wasn't a friend to him, I thought. Anybody's first line of defense is a best friend. Mom is Dad's best friend. Lynn is Ben's best friend. I should be turning into Michael's best friend.

It caught at me.

Michael, not Annie, was to be my best friend. Michael—or some other boy—would last forever. Not Annie.

"It was my fault," I said. "You put a lot of work into that. Don't you think Eliza is going to turn out to be fascinating? But listen, I can worry about Eliza another time. Once when we were in the computer store, the salesman was working out everybody's first name in huge fat block letters. You remember that? Each letter took up a single page. He filled in the blocks with little s's. I'd love to have your name written out like that. I'd hang it on my bedroom wall."

Michael said it was a cinch to do that and would take only moments. The moments lasted longer, because I put on some rock music and we kept interrupting the programming to dance. Finally he had a perfect M-I-C-H-A-E-L, seven feet long. He did not make the letters black with s's. He filled them in with tiny *fraser-fraser-fraser-fraser*'s.

When school began Monday, Chapman High had never seemed so large. I was too tired for the stairs, too worn out for the classes. I could barely remember what my schedule was, and when Mr. McGrath asked for the history paper outlines, I realized with a sinking heart that Michael and I had partied all weekend. I had never gone to any library at all.

There are some good things about being known as a brain. Even Mr. McGrath assumes that Fraser Mac-Kendrick is about to get 800 on her college boards any minute now. Sure enough, he accepted a very feeble excuse and agreed that I could have another week to do my outline. I felt slightly sick at misrepresenting myself, especially when he refused the excuses of two other kids whose reasons were doubtless more valid than mine.

We had a substitute in gym, and because the heating system wasn't working properly and the sub was a hundred pounds overweight, we didn't have to dress out. I sagged on the locker-room bench while the talk of the other girls swirled around me.

Connie had broken her New Year's resolution 83 times in two months. Everyone giggled. "Chocolate," explained Connie. "I wasn't going to eat it again."

"You should have resolved that in reverse," said Julie. "If you'd resolved to eat chocolate daily, you could have kept your resolution. Now you've got both chocolate and guilt."

"Speaking of guilt," said Smedes, "we had to put my grandfather in a nursing home last week. We can't keep him with us any more because of his medical condition. He's angry at us and thinks we don't love him any more. He cried when we left him at the nursing home. It was horrible."

Smedes, like me, bears an ancient maiden name. (I must say I find Fraser more acceptable than Smedes, however.) Everybody sympathized with Smedes, and we talked of families and their duties to each other. Connie broke in to say that she was having a chocolate attack, so we thoughtfully ate her chocolate kisses for her, to prevent another lapse.

Julie said she had read a terrific book called *Ordinary People* where the teen-age boy is trying not to attempt suicide a second time. "Julie," said Smedes, "how could a plot like that possibly be good?"

"Really, it was," said Julie. "It was a high school just like Chapman and kids just like us, and parents just like ours. You should read it."

Ordinary People, I thought. I can remember that title. I haven't read much in months. If Julie recommends it, it's good.

Somebody had lost an earring. Somebody else found it for her. Smedes had to borrow a dollar for lunch money. Connie said, "Did you hear about the kid who fell downstairs and is in a coma?"

"No," I said, horrified. "Somebody at the high school?"

"No. Younger, I think. Just an ordinary fall downstairs, you'd expect a few bruises, but she fell head first and she's been unconscious for quite a while."

"The poor parents," exclaimed Smedes. "Think how guilty *they* must feel. Letting their kid horse around near the stairs. They must be going through hell right now."

I hate hearing about injured children. I hate hearing the sirens of ambulances, and whenever I have to pull over to let an ambulance pass me I start to feel sick myself. I don't know if it's identification with the victim inside, or guilt that I'm okay, or fear, or what. Connie was toying with her last chocolate kiss. She didn't eat it, and nobody asked for it. I suppose we all half felt that you couldn't go around happily chomping on chocolate when other people were dying. Smedes said, "How's your research project going, Fraser?"

"I love it. A fantastic exciting girl named Eliza Lucas Pinckney."

"Just think," said Smedes. "If your ancestor or mine had been Pinckney, we'd be named Pinckney instead of Smedes or Fraser." Smedes looked at me carefully. "Yes, I think you'd be an ideal Pinckney," she said. "Hereafter, I'm going to address you as Pinckney."

"Not if you value your life," I said.

After school I rushed to the library to concentrate on Eliza. It felt queer to be there without doing Toybrary. I felt as if I were taking wrong turns, doing something illegal, heading into adult reference.

I looked up *indigo* in a book on natural dyes. There was a page of color photographs and for the first time I saw the color of indigo. A wonderful blue. Suddenly I saw Eliza, sixteen and slender, like me, but wearing a dress of indigo blue, sweeping past her white-pillared mansion, ducking under a wisteria vine, going to check her live oaks and her silk worms, her flax and her hemp. Oh, Eliza! I thought. What a woman you were!

"Fraser?" said Miss Herschel.

I looked up. She was visibly upset. I forgot to tell people not to call me at the library, I thought. But it isn't Toybrary day. Nobody knows I'm here.

"Did you hear the news, Fraser?"

"No, what?" Good. She wasn't mad at me about phone calls. Probably some new donation for Toybrary. I could not care less what anybody gives Toybrary, I thought. I have outgrown it. I have to apply myself and find another girl to run it.

"Kit Lipton," said Miss Herschel. "Remember that cute little girl with the brown hair who always bounced?"

"My favorite patron," I said. "A Barbie Doll fiend who recently turned to Science instead." I smiled to myself, wondering how the Sun Graphics Kit had worked out for her.

"She had a terrible fall. She's in a coma. She's probably dying."

Chapter 8

Hospitals overwhelm me.

It seems impossible that I ever cared about term papers or hairstyles, boy friends or Madrigals, when I smell that peculiar sick scent of newly washed hospital floors, see the orderlies pushing a stretcher down the hall to X-ray, watch an elderly sick man attempt to maneuver a walker, listen to nervous families in the waiting room aching for news.

I don't think I want a medical career. It must be very consuming, because I don't see how you would ever get over that feeling that nothing else matters. Your whole existence would be so many iron filings drawn inexorably to the magnet of the hospital.

And yet, once I'm inside hospital doors, all I do

want is a medical career, because what else matters, except pain and death and healing?

I took the elevator to the fourth floor and walked slowly down the hall to the nurses' station to check in. Kit's room was not open to casual visitors. I had had to phone her parents to ask them to put me on an allowed-visitors list. It was a horrible phone call. Mr. and Mrs. Lipton could not speak without choking up. They told me how Kit had been dancing. She had gotten a tutu for Christmas and was pirouetting all over the house, and they had even said to her, "Don't go close to the stairs," but they didn't actually move to stop her, and she lost her balance and fell as they watched, head first to the bottom floor.

The nurse smiled at me. "Kit's having some treatments now," she explained. "You wait in the sitting room. Mr. and Mrs. Lipton are there. They'll be relieved to have company."

Oh, no. Would we sit awkwardly in those ugly red vinyl seats, flipping through ancient magazines? Would I tell them about high school this year while we all tried not to think of Kit? But there was no place else to go, and the nurse was watching, so I trekked another fifteen feet down the hall and turned into the tiny ugly visitors' room. It really felt like a trek. It might even be easier to walk across a veldt than to approach the parents of a dying child.

They were both weeping.

"Hi," I said, and the syllable felt too light and carefree, but I could not think of the proper greeting. "I'm Fraser MacKendrick."

"Oh, Fraser!" cried Mrs. Lipton. She was a little

woman and rather dumpy. When she hugged me I had to bend over so that her face wasn't in my sleeve. She used a wrinkled Kleenex to dry her tears. "I'm so glad to meet you at last, Fraser. Kit came home every Thursday from Toybrary and told us about you, and of course when you phoned and wanted to visit Kit, we wanted you to, even though she isn't aware of anything right now."

"Has she improved any?" I said anxiously.

Mrs. Lipton bit her upper lip. It was a thin lip and lacked color, and it was chapped. "No," she said in a voice like her lips, and we all began crying.

They told me every medical detail, but not in order of chronology or anatomy—in the order of its shock to them. They told me what it was like at home, with Kit's little brother still an infant and needing sitters, responsible sitters, every time they drove the thirty miles into the city medical center.

Their pain poured out of them like liquid. Neither of them could stop. If Mrs. Lipton took a breath, Mr. Lipton began. He was a very plain man. I could not imagine Kit—laughing, joyous, celebrating Kit—as the daughter of these two dull and dumpy people. Maybe Kit was the light of their lives, I thought, and without her there's no spark to them at all.

"And the money," said Mrs. Lipton. "Oh, dear God in heaven. I don't know what we're going to do about the money."

"Surely there's insurance," I said. There would be tens of thousands of dollars in medical bills if they had no insurance.

"For the medical bills, yes," said Mr. Lipton. "My company has an excellent policy for that. Kit's completely covered. No, it's our expenses that we're not going to be able to meet. Do you realize that just driving in and out of the city uses half a tank of gas? That parking fees for an entire day in that lot are as much as we usually spend on food? That we have to hire a baby-sitter for Jonathan, and adult sitters charge a fortune? We just don't have that kind of extra money. I'm not some lawyer or physician. I drive a delivery van for a bakery. They're being good; they're letting me take all these days as sick days, so I'm still getting paid. But we just aren't going to be able to afford to visit Kit."

Both my parents had good jobs, and they had only me left to support, and yet we were still trying to figure out how to buy another car. What would it be like, dealing with the added expenses like Kit's visitation, on what would have to be a very low income as a driver for a bakery? I drove Sunday mornings for the florist. They couldn't possibly be paying Mr. Lipton very much.

"That's terrible," I said. "Isn't there some way— some loan—some group in town? Maybe your church or something?"

"You don't want to beg for money," said Mrs. Lipton. "It makes you sick. And anyway, the money isn't really for Kit. Kit's taken care of. It's for us. For stupid things like parking-lot fees. I can't ask a charity for that."

We talked for an hour. I should say, they talked. I have never been with people who needed a listener as much as they did.

In the end I caught only a glimpse of Kit. Her parents began crying again the moment they saw her in bed; white and thin and already corpselike, but with the horrid additions of tubes everywhere, and her eyes closed and bruised. Mrs. Lipton began talking in a quavery voice, as if Kit could hear, "And on television last night, honey, on your favorite show, guess what happened? Well, first—"

I slipped out. The tears were coming so hard for me I could hardly navigate down the hall. The charge nurse handed me a few Kleenex and said, "Now don't start driving home until you're under control. We don't want a second body in here."

A body. That's what Kit was. A body.

"You went by yourself to see that little girl?" said Michael. He was very quiet. We were in Vinnie's, and the only booth available was near the door, so constant blasts of chilly air and the ring of the cash register and the laughter of the waitresses bothered us.

"You didn't know her, Michael. But she was very special to me." I'm using the past tense, I thought. Oh, Fraser, stop it, she's not dead yet, she might live, sometimes they come out of their comas, you could jinx it. I thought, nonsense, there's no such thing as a jinx. "*Is* special," I said.

Michael sipped a Pepsi. He wasn't looking at me. He was staring down into his glass. "I'd have driven you, Fray."

"I didn't think it involved you. It was something I had to do alone."

"I enjoy doing things with you," he said.

I snapped at him. "There was nothing enjoyable about visiting a little girl who's still unconscious after a week and will probably die."

"I didn't mean that. Fraser, please don't—please relax. I'm not your enemy, okay? I meant that I'd have gone along. Don't you think it would have been easier with company?"

"No," I said.

Michael still didn't look at me. He picked up the paper mat in front of him that said Vinnie's and listed the menu and the local sights of interest, and he folded it into a paper airplane. "I wish I knew why you keep getting so irritable with me," he said. "I almost asked Judith to tell me about hormones and stuff, but I decided not to."

I was outraged. We were talking about Kit dying, and he was there making paper airplanes and talking hormones. "There is nothing hormonal about getting irritated with you," I said furiously, keeping my shout to a whisper so the entire restaurant wouldn't overhear. "And there's no reason to bring Judith into anything. You want to know about periods? You want to know about menstruation? You want a physiology lecture?"

Michael blanched. "No. We had health in seventh grade and that was enough for me. I'm just trying to understand, Fraser. It seems to me every time I do the right thing, it's the wrong thing. Like visiting Kit. You went and drove your folks both to work and fussed around getting an official class cut so you could drive into the city and back before you had to get your father and mother from work. But Fraser, if you'd told me, I'd have borrowed Judith's car and taken you and there wouldn't have been a fraction of the trouble. It's like you driving up to the University Library without telling me. I'd have taken you. But no. The day after you visited Kit, you didn't even call me. You just left. I phoned your house Saturday morning, and your mother says,

Oh, didn't Fraser tell you? She's going to do research and won't be back till after supper."

Saturday had been a queer day. Half of me was fascinated by Eliza and thrilled by the college atmosphere. Eliza was more interesting than anybody could have guessed, and every time I glanced at all the college kids I got a tingle of excitement knowing I would be one of them, right here, in another year. But half of me was in agony, remembering Kit at every page turn, thinking, *Will she die? And if she lives, will there be brain damage?*

One poor little girl, who was dancing around at the top of the stairs and lost her balance. Oh, God, surely she deserves another chance to dance. Please God let her be all right.

I would read more about Eliza. About how she married Mr. Pinckney, whom she had adored from afar for years, and how she raised a son who became a signer of the Constitution of the United States.

And I would think, Kit could be an Eliza. Kit had— *has, has*—potential. Character. Determination. Don't let her die, God. If You go and let her die, I won't forgive You.

And I would think of all children in the world who don't have a chance, and all the terrible wars I researched last year that were still going on, and all the deaths that shouldn't be. Tears would drip onto the page about Southern plantation life and wrinkle the paper in curly bubbles.

It was Annie I wanted to talk to. But I couldn't reach Annie. Literally. Every time I telephoned, her mother told me Annie was off with Price somewhere. I felt like a person dialing 911 in an emergency and the line was busy.

I talked to my mother, but she can't bear to hear about children who die young. She kept shivering and saying, "I'm sure the child will be all right, Fraser, let's just don't worry so much."

I wanted to talk about motherhood and childbirth and nurturing and all the things that Mrs. Lipton had done for Kit and what was the point? Where had it all led, if Kit was to die at age seven?

But there was no one, so I kept it inside.

Michael pummeled the ice shards at the bottom of his glass with a straw, as if it were a jackhammer. The straw bent like a broken leg. "I don't see why you don't come to me first," he said. "Isn't that what this is all about?"

We were sitting across from each other, which was a mistake. We couldn't snuggle, we could only look into the angry features opposite. "What is what all about?" I said. I knew I was starting a fight. I knew I was being unfair.

"Us," said Michael.

"Has nothing to do with Kit Lipton," I said. I felt better, being obnoxious. What's the matter with me? I thought.

"It seems to me you're too emotional over everything," said Michael.

"*Too* emotional? A little girl I liked very much may die any hour and I'm *too* emotional?"

Michael set his jaw. He was wearing a heavy wool shirt, and the collar hadn't been ironed; it kept flapping, and each time he turned his head from me in anger, the collar point scraped his cheek and he had to shove it down. Another time, a more loving time, I'd have walked around the booth and gotten in next to him and tucked the collar inside his pullover sweater so it would lie quietly. Now I was perversely glad that at least something was bothering Michael.

"You're the first girl I've dated for any length of time, Fraser," said Michael at last. He was so fidgety he could hardly sit there. I knew he wanted to drive off and abandon me. Only the fact that I would have no way to get home was preventing him. "I admit I don't understand. I admit I have different attitudes than you do about a lot of things, but—"

"All you care about is *you*!" I said fiercely. "Have you even asked me how Kit is? No. All you care about is who drove the car. Have you asked whether I got lots of research done? No. All you care about is I didn't have your permission to do it."

"That's not true," he said. "You didn't need permission. I'm not some creep who expects you to have my consent every time you turn around. I'm just dating you, Fraser. I want to spend time with you. Especially Saturdays. Especially free afternoons. It seems to me that common courtesy—"

"See? You *still* didn't ask about Kit."

Michael sank back. His face became absolutely immobile. His breathing was so controlled I could not see his chest rise or fall. "Okay," he said quietly. "How is Kit?"

But I didn't tell him. I kept the fight going. I said, "What, I have to give you orders to get you to exhibit a little concern?"

He ceased to look in my direction at all. He began folding and refolding the paper airplane, pressing the creases down with his thumb nail and then reversing the fold.

Oh, Michael, I thought, I'm not angry with you. I think I'm angry with God, for letting Kit fall down stairs. Maybe I'm really angry with Kit, for being clumsy. Maybe I'm angry at my mother for being afraid to talk about death, or at Annie for being too busy to consider what happened.

The anger seeped out of me. We sat silently in the booth, exhausted. I told myself to make an effort to repair things, but I didn't. I told myself to touch his hand and let the power of touch start the repairs, but I didn't reach out.

"Hey, what do you know?" Price boomed in my ear. "Told you we'd find them here, Annie." Price slipped in next to me, and I had to shift over to make room for him. Annie sat next to Michael. She was flushed with pleasure. It was fairly warm out; spring was approaching; her light jacket was unzipped, and she was a riot of colors—a rainbow sweater, an electric-blue jacket.

"It's Monday," I said to Annie. "How come you're not at your violin lesson?"

"I'm only taking every other week now," she said. "It was getting to be too much to keep up with."

If I had been sitting on the outside of the booth I'd have left. I would just have started walking, even though it was miles. But I was fenced in by Price, and by my former best friend, and by Michael.

My former best friend.

Their talk swirled around me. Two people having fun. One struggling to regain his equilibrium. And me, completely removed.

Annie was no longer my best friend.

In a dark booth at Vinnie's, part of my life ended.

The other half of that life didn't even notice. She had become half of a couple, a piece of Price Quincy; and if there wasn't enough left for her violin, there certainly wasn't enough left for me.

"Listen," said Price, as if we had any choice, with his loud sharp voice. "This time my father managed to get four tickets to the ice-hockey game. Last one of the season. Two fantastic teams. It should be wild."

"I hate ice hockey," I said. "It's too violent."

"But they choose to be violent," said Michael. "They know they're going to lose a few teeth and they figure it's worth it in order to play. It's not like war on innocent civilians, Fraser. Those guys want to be out there bashing each other's heads as often as the puck."

Annie said, "Price and I went and it wasn't as bad as I thought, Fray. Hardly any blood at all. And the rest of the game is really exciting."

"Oh, Annie!" I cried, at the worst posible time, in the worst posible company. "I can't bear how you've changed. What happened to you? How can you be like this?"

There was a long silence.

Price and Annie just looked at me. Blankly. It was a mark of how our friendship had dissolved that Annie did not know what I was talking about. Michael said, "She's upset about Kit Lipton, that's all."

It wasn't all, but I was glad he had rescued me. It was a good excuse for saying something ugly; it would absolve me.

"Did you get in to see her?" said Annie. "I heard they weren't allowing visitors or I'd have tried to go, too."

"I called her parents for special permission. They

remembered me from Toybrary and agreed. Kit looks awful. Lying there like a frozen bundle of arms and legs, perforated with tubes and monitors. She looks dead already."

Michael's hand went across the table to me and we clasped fingers. Mine were cold, his warm. I marveled at the power of touch.

"Oh, Fraser," he said. "No wonder you feel so rotten."

Annie said, "I wish there were something we could do. I feel so helpless. Doctors can't help, though, so neither can I. Price, this little girl was such a sweetheart. So bouncy. When she took a toy from Toybrary she hugged it to her heart as if it were the answer to her prayers. We adored Kit."

Price nodded. "I'm not that crazy about little kids," he said. "I'm just as glad you're not involved with Toybrary any more. It must have been boring."

"Well, it was in a way," said Annie. "Where are the seats at the Coliseum, Price? Are they good ones?"

"You kidding? Would my father get crumby tickets?"

Annie giggled. "Of course not."

I've lost my best friend, I thought again.

In Toybrary, I watch a lot of little boys and girls. Boys never chatter. They exchange, they demand, they argue, they leave. But girls are apt to share emotions. Even when a toy is popular with both sexes—say, an old-fashioned toy, like the wonderful wooden Pinocchio marionette—the boys simply bring it back and set it down, whereas the girls tell you how they put on a little play. They'll even discuss the theme of the play— like say, getting lost and being found.

Boys seemed to me more essentially alone. Girls knew early on that good friends made a good toy or a good thought better.

Kit probably had a good friend, I thought. Katurah is probably angling for one, too. Katurah probably already knows that an older brother is all very well, but what a girl needs as her first line of defense is a friend. At Katurah's age, friends wouldn't share anything more important than broken crayons, but she'd be in training for the day when she had hoards of little girl friends and out of that hoard would come one, as Annie had come to me, just to talk to.

My mother and I have had the worst fights in our family, but we've had the best times, too. With my father, everything is so brief, so quickly summarized. He thinks a subject should be discussed once and then neatly packaged with a closing ribbon like "You'll grow out of this, Fraser"; "You won't even remember this next year, Fraser"; "Everybody feels that way, Fraser." And then he believes the topic is closed.

But nothing is ever closed. No wound heals completely. The hurt of being left out, the shame of publicly failing, the ache of knowing that you're not expert enough to get what you want in a school with so much competition—these don't go away easily. The wounds need to be tended to. That's what a best friend is for. Tending.

That night I cried myself to sleep.

But I did not know if I was weeping for Kit, dying in a big-city medical center. Or for a friendship that was slipping away before I could catch it. Or for my own confusion over Michael—my never-fail technique at ripping apart the only good relationship I had ever had with a boy.

Chapter 9

It was a second Wednesday—for years, Needle N Thread night at our house. But now Mom was home. "Mom?" I said.

"Yes, dear."

"Don't you miss Needle N Thread?" I'll get her talking about her friends, I thought. Then we'll move into talking about Annie. About what's happened. About whether I'm the one who's crazy or Annie is. I won't aim for talking about Kit tonight; Mom can't handle that.

"Yes, I do," she said. "It was an awful lot of fun. After all these years, we knew each other so well. You can be so much more productive sitting around, talking, while you do your needlework. I always felt sort of warm. Sort of Early American. Like a quilting bee."

"But Mom, if you liked it so much, why did you quit?"

We were in the kitchen. Our kitchen was poorly designed. It has one long wasted wall with no counters, no space for a table to press up, no shelves because the corridor effect is too narrow. My mother wanted it to be an interesting wall, to make up for being a stupid wall. For years she bought old mirrors at tag and antique sales. She has seventeen large, and I don't know how many small, mirrors on that wall. Old primitive frames and narrow curlicued frames, speckled black reflections and quivery old glass. I looked at my mother and myself over and over, different sizes and angles in the mirrors. It made me queasy.

"Well, your father is home. If I have a choice, I like to be with your father."

"But he's just watching television. You're in here making tomorrow's dinner ahead."

"Well, I don't literally have to be in his arms, Fraser. It's just nice being together. I like being home when he's home."

"But don't you miss your friends?"

"Not that much, really. I have your father."

I tried to think of Michael like that. I have Michael. So I don't need anything else. I don't need to sing in Madrigals, I don't need to take walks alone in the country, I don't need to browse in libraries, I don't need Annie.

I stared at my mother. She didn't notice. I turned and watched her in the mirrors instead, and this time she was aware of my gaze and twinkled her fingers at me. Dozens of me twinkled back. "Some of those are pretty messy," she said, handing me Windex and paper towels. "I can't imagine why I thought mirrors were a perfect decoration for a wall close to the stove. Oh, well."

I polished mirrors.

The phone rang. "It's Michael," called my father.

I took the call in the front hallway, instead of up in my bedroom the way I always do, for privacy. My father looked at me strangely, but he walked away carefully, closing the doors to give me privacy anyhow. "Hi, Michael," I said.

"Hi. Listen. Don't you want to change your mind about the hockey game? Price's father got fantastic seats. Right near the front."

How could I explain to him enough times that right near the front was the last place I would want to be if I went to a hockey game, which I didn't want to do? "No, thanks."

He sighed. "Okay."

Silence. A pain sharper than cramps shot through me, and my throat got hot and tight. *I love you, Michael.* "Couldn't you let Price have both our tickets," I said, "and we'll do something else?"

"Fraser, when do I ever get to go to a pro hockey game? With seats like this? I don't want to do anything else."

"I do."

"Yes, you've made your point very clearly. Okay. I'll see you next week then. You can research Eliza, since you get such a thrill out of being alone in a library." He hung up.

Michael, whose patience was what first attracted me to him! Whose sweetness with Katurah was so nice to see! Michael, exasperated beyond belief with me! I could imagine him, the way his eyes would be closing. The way his large smooth hand would tug at his hair, pulling it back as if he could pull the frown off his forehead. How his eyes would open very slowly, so that for him the room must materialize by degrees, and he'd take a long deep breath, his wide chest spreading wider, pulling the cables of his gray sweater taut, and then relaxing.

Oh, Michael!

I kept on Windexing mirrors, and polishing them far more carefully than my mother's standards required, and it caught at me again—pain like a fishhook; fear like a tightening wire.

I want to have Michael. If these are the demands he makes, I have to go with it.

I called him back. "Michael? I'll go."

The Coliseum stank of beer and sweat and popcorn. It was jammed with more men than women, all wearing dark, heavy clothes, all overly eager. All I could think of was Romans gathering at their Coliseum for their games; slaughters and blood and thumbs down for death. When the teams skated out, the spectators bellowed things like "Get 'em, Billy!" and "Kill 'em, Nick!"

This is how I choose to spend my time? I thought. Kit is dying and I'm sitting here waiting to see these people attack one another?

"Now just relax, Fraser," said Michael. He handed me a Coke, and it sat in my hand cold and heavy. "It's fun, really," he told me. "It's just a game, like basketball. You love basketball. Make an effort and you'll love this too."

I'll never like it, I thought. The game hasn't even started and I want to leave. I hate the whole audience. I hate myself for being here. I hate Annie for giggling and shouting. "Michael, I want to go home." I said.

"We all came in Price's van," Michael said. "You can hardly drive away. You know what? The first time we double-dated and picked up that log cabin, I figured Price was the one who was going to be the problem. But I was wrong. You are."

"I'm taking a taxi to the bus stop," I said, "and taking the bus back to Chapman."

"You can't do that," said Michael fiercely, and his fingers dug into my arm. "The bus stop is in the worst section of town. You shouldn't even get *out* of a taxi there, let alone wait for a bus. Now just shut up and cooperate, Fraser. We're here now, and if you didn't want to come you shouldn't have come."

He was right. The bus station was out of the question. And so I sat, while the spectators around me screamed. It was the most involved audience I had ever come across. It made college football look like nursery school. People shrieked encouragement, and when they jumped up they stomped on their beer cans to flatten them. Michael yelled right along with them, and so did Price.

And so did Annie.

On the covers of the paperback romances Annie and I used to read there would be a blurb. *As David sweeps Cathy away . . . Read how Lance sweeps the resentful Mignonette into the oblivion of love . . .*

It really meant that. Annie had been swept away. You could not even tell now where she had stood. No footprints on the carpet pile, no scuff marks on the floor. Price had swept her away. Price was still there. But Annie was not.

"Miss Fraser MacKendrick, please," said a thin metallic voice.

I could not imagine who was on the phone. It sounded very official. What applications had I made (or serious criminal errors!) that would lead to an official phone call? A total stranger always assumed that Fraser MacKendrick was a boy and addressed me as "Mr." I said dubiously, "This is Fraser MacKendrick."

"Hold the line for Lacy Buckley," said the metallic voice, now sounding slightly rusty.

"Lacy Buckley!" I said.

Lacy ran the morning talk show. The national talk show carried most of the hour, but she did the local segments. I'd been on Lacy's show twice when I was kicking off Toybrary. Being on television was nothing like what I had expected, and being on Lacy's was more fun than any of the others, because she was actually interested. The rest were just killing time.

Lacy looked somewhat like my mother. She was my height, but stocky. She wore blouses to match her name—silk, festooned with miles of lace. She had an oddly shaped nose, a big mouth over a sagging chin; long, flat eyebrows, and hair skinned back into a tight bun skewered with pins and draped with ribbons.

All this, and yet she was a striking, altogether appealing woman. I was crazy about her.

She remembered me, I thought. How fantastic.

"Fraser?" said her familiar voice. Big and chunky, like a necklace nobody would ever really wear in public, her voice thrust itself into your living room and never left.

"Hello, Lacy," I said joyously. "How are you?" She was one of the first adults I ever addressed by her first name. She had told me to, and it felt comfortable.

"Splendid, my dear. It's almost one year since you launched Toybrary. We want to schedule a first-anniversary interview. Be prepared with statistics about toy use. What toys are popular. How many you own now. What types. How many children are actually patrons of Toybrary. That sort of thing."

I had kept plenty of statistics. More for something to do than for any future purpose. But the notebook that Annie and I kept in the desk drawer had all that. I'd just have to add it up. Make lists.

"I'll want you in here Thursday morning at eight-thirty. You don't have a conflicting class, do you?"

Of course I had a conflicting class. Thursday is a school day. Counting on my *she's a brain and this is good publicity* status, I said, "No problem. I'll be there at eight-thirty."

"Splendid." She left the phone without saying goodbye, and since it was my third time with her, I knew enough not to hang up myself. The metallic-voiced secretary would come on with instructions. "Miss MacKendrick? We'd advise wearing bright clothing, some eye makeup, but no more than you usually wear, and get here at quarter after eight rather than eight-thirty. Got it?"

"Got it."

"Splendid," said the voice in puny imitation of Lacy.

And it was. There's nothing like being sought after for television to make you feel good!

Michael drove me into the city to see Kit again.

He was very careful. He was careful driving in city traffic; he was careful to keep the radio tuned to my favorite station; and he was careful to discuss Kit, the whole Kit and nothing but Kit. No way was he going to have me accuse him of being unfeeling this time.

Of course, this time I wanted to talk about us, not Kit. What was there to say about her now, that we had not already said? A little girl still comatose—nearly a month now—no more signs of life than before—no improvements whatsoever. Two weeping parents, tears still coming from ducts that must be wearing thin from overuse.

I was not sure why I kept going in to see her. Because that's what it was, really. I saw her. I didn't speak to her, comfort her, or give her anything. Nor did she give me anything. I just walked in and looked at her for a while. Sometimes I felt like a spectator at the hockey game—waiting for my share of the action. Don't die while I'm here, Kit, I would think, watching the pitiful slight movement under the sheets that passed for breathing.

Michael wasn't on the list of allowed visitors. I stood alone in Kit's room, watching the liquid drop from the I.V. bottle and seep slowly into her veins. Her nose was filled with tubes, and her mouth was slack. The missing teeth had grown in. The teeth had kept right on growing, no matter that Kit wasn't around to be aware of it, and filled in the gaps. She looked strangely older lying there without her baby gaps.

Please God let her play with Barbie Dolls again, I thought. Or let her be a scientist.

What are You up to, God? What's Your theory here?

But no answers came.

I went back to the ugly waiting room to get Michael. He was leafing through a seven-month-old *Time* Magazine. Across from him was Mrs. Lipton. She shocked me. Like Kit, she had aged. But unlike Kit, she looked like a hag. This is the mother of a newborn infant? I thought, remembering little Jonathan. She looks like a great-grandmother. "Hello, Mrs. Lipton," I said.

"Oh, Fraser!" she cried. And I mean cried. Even a single syllable turned to tears for her.

And once again the same things poured out of her. Not so much about Kit, because she had said it all, but about the money. "We can't afford it, Fraser. We can't come again till next Saturday. I can't pay a baby-sitter any more, and I used up the last dollar in our savings account. I literally don't have another cent until Jack's payday next Friday."

I'm not good at comforting people. I don't know what to say to them. I felt despicable having money when she didn't. But what could I do? Open my purse, hand her my ten dollars left from the florist and say, here, come tomorrow with this?

I opened my purse and gave her the ten dollars left from the florist and said, "Here. Come with this."

"Oh, no, Fraser. Absolutely not. We can't go begging. If I had realized how you would react, I wouldn't have said these things. Now listen, honey, enough of my problems. You tell me about Toybrary. How's it going these days?" She managed a reasonable facsimile

111

of a smile, so I gave her one in exchange, furtively tucking the ten dollars back in my bag. "It's great. I've almost talked two sophomore girls into taking it over for me, and next week I'm going to be on Lacy Buckley's show talking about what the first year has been like."

"How exciting," exclaimed Mrs. Lipton. "You've been on television before. I know, because Kit saw you one morning when she was home with the flu. What's it like?"

So I told her what it was like. The huge cameras, big as washing machines on movable pedestals, and the great cables lying on the floors. The peculiar fake two-sided room in the middle of an area as large as a school gym. How Lacy sat in a comfy rocking chair with a good back, and her guest sat on fat ploppy upholstered seats, where they sank in so deep they were trapped and couldn't escape any of Lacy's questions, ever.

"I feel so cheered talking to you, Fraser," said Mrs. Lipton, and she looked cheered. I could even see a little of Kit in her; some of the verve. "Now you have a good time on that show and wear something green, like you have on today. Green is such a good color for you." She stretched up to kiss my cheek and walked briskly down the hall to visit her daughter.

I was glad she was cheered. I myself felt drained. It was as if the act of cheering Mrs. Lipton had sucked the cheer out of me. I stood limply, thinking of nothing, just recuperating.

"You didn't tell me you were going to be on TV."

I had forgotten Michael. I turned, jarred. "Oh," I said.

"Yes. *Oh.* It's me. Michael Hollander. Remember? The guy who drove you here?"

"Don't let's fight." I said tiredly, reaching for my jacket and walking toward the exit.

He caught up with me. "I wasn't fighting, Fraser. I was just mentioning that you didn't mention being on television to me. It's pretty important. I would have thought you'd tell me about it when we were driving in."

I pressed the elevator button. It was very large, a translucent white, shaped like an obese arrow, for people who can't read UP or DOWN. I'm one, I thought. I'm so tired I need that arrow to be sure where I'm going.

You find the perfect man, I thought, but now you cease to be the perfect woman. You become a shaving off his stick. You eat his candy, play his games. *He sweeps you away.* If you're Lynn, you take up sailing. If you're Mom, you take up genealogy, surrender Needle N Thread. If you're Annie, you take up sports, surrender violin. If you're Judith you take up stamps, surrender owl prowls.

"Michael," I said.

The elevator door opened. We got in. There was a technician leaning against the back, holding a tray full of vials of blood.

"What?" said Michael. He pushed the ground-floor button.

"I think we should break up."

Michael froze. He didn't close his eyes, the way I expected. He didn't look angry or upset. He simply became stiff. He turned very slowly toward me, as if some military officer had given an order to attention. He said absolutely nothing and didn't look as if he planned on saying anything.

113

The doors opened at the ground floor. We got out. The technician stayed in and the doors closed.

I put on my jacket. Michael helped me with the left sleeve. I dropped my purse and Michael picked it up. "Thank you," I said. I got to the door first and pushed it part way; Michael pushed it the rest. We walked silently across the large lot to where we had parked Judith's Datsun. "I'll pay the parking fee," I said, retrieving the ticket from the dashboard. We weren't staying all day like Mrs. Lipton; our fee was the minimum $2.50. Michael took the money and handed it to the gatekeeper.

When we were out of the city, on the Interstate, he said, "Is Kit any better?"

"No change, really."

"Her parents sure have financial troubles."

"Yes."

"It was nice of you to offer to help."

I shrugged. "I guess it was rude. She couldn't take charity like that. Not face to face."

We didn't talk during the rest of the drive. When we got there, Ben's car was parked out front. Everybody was home. "Thanks for driving me," I said. My stomach hurt again. I didn't want to cry in front of Michael either. I wanted to save it for later. In my bedroom, under the covers, in the comfort of my pillowcase.

He said, "You definitely want to break up?" His voice was cramped, as if he weren't getting enough air.

I have to give him a reason, I thought. I can't just give him his marching orders. It isn't nice. But what do I tell him? Michael, you drown me? Michael, sometimes I can't bear the sight of you? Michael, I detest all your hobbies? I said, "It isn't you, Michael."

114

"Then who is it?"

Oh, God. Now he thought I had some other, better boy stashed away. When I was beginning to wonder how I would ever get along with *any* boy. Ever. "No one," I said. "I mean, me. It's me. There's something wrong with me."

The excuse felt all right. It was always all right to take the blame. My mother did it all the time. No matter that Dad was driving us crazy, she made herself look dumb in order to stop it. She never blamed him. "There really isn't any reason, Michael. It's just me. I don't think I get along with people very well. I think I'm selfish." I ran myself down for a while, until I no longer felt I was throwing Michael away. I felt like a rotten person who didn't deserve Michael.

When I was finally able to look at him, his eyes were fixed on Ben's car. "Okay," he said.

We had spent six months of our lives with each other. Inseparable, sharing our lives, our hours, our activities. Okay, you want to break up? Okay. It's all the same to me.

"But thank you," I said. I couldn't quite make myself get out of the car, and yet I wanted to fly, to run, to be away from him before I changed my mind and submitted again.

"You're welcome," he said, giving me a tight smile, ducking his head in a way that reminded me strangely of Annie, and my tears began. I got out of the car quickly before they showed on my cheeks.

Chapter 10

"The most popular toys are different for boys and girls," I said into Lacy's eyes. They tell you to look at the interviewer and never at the camera. It's quite hard to do when three massive cameras are bearing down on you. "Boys tend to like things that move. Cars, trucks, tanks, weapons. Girls . . ."

Lacy dislikes anything that claims boys and girls are different. I can't imagine why. If there is one thing I have learned, it is that boys and girls are very different. She cut me off and changed subjects. "Is there much call for the really large objects?" she said. "The five-foot Teddy bear? The log cabin?"

"Oh, yes. In fact, we took reserves on the log cabin and we're booked right through September."

How do you pick up a log cabin? said Michael. I'm a weight lifter and I'd be hard-pressed to pick up a log cabin.

"And do the toys with many pieces—the Legos, the knights-and-castles sets—usually come back with every piece?" asked Lacy.

"We've never had any trouble with missing pieces. The children hate borrowing anything with a piece missing so they're very careful to bring it back with every item in its proper place."

I had found two girls to take over Toybrary. Ginny and Leigh. Sophomores. I didn't like them much. They made it clear they were only doing Toybrary in order to have something terrific to put on their college applications. They didn't care much about kids or about toys; they just wanted an activity.

I answered two more questions. It was my third time with her, my fifth time on television. I was much more relaxed. There's no audience. Just me and Lacy, invisible cameramen and women, and a whole staff of people at lights and microphones and desks and headsets.

I thought, But I'm no different from Ginny and Leigh. Why did I do Toybrary? Just for something to do. Just because the idea came and I was there.

"So what plans are ahead for you now, Fraser?" said Lacy, beaming. "What activity—what fascinating thing are you going to arrange now?"

The strangest thing happened.

I began telling her something I had not had a single thought about until that moment. Not once had these thoughts gone through my conscious mind. And yet there they were—formed, ready, articulate, prepared. I wondered if Kit's mind was at work, too, in some inner recess medical science was ignorant about.

"I'm starting the Kit Lipton Fund," I said. "Kit is a seven-year-old girl from Chapman who came every week to Toybrary. She was a pretty little kid, brown hair, crooked teeth, and we liked her a lot because she was so thrilled with everything she took out. Kit got a lot of excitement out of life and it was fun to be around her. She sparkled."

Lacy hasn't been on television for twenty years without learning to recognize a cue line. She leaned forward, looking concerned. "What happened to Kit, Fraser?"

"She fell down the stairs. A perfectly ordinary tumble, except that she's been in a coma for weeks now. Her parents have medical insurance to cover her expenses, but they have no money to cover their own. They can't even visit her now, because they have no savings left to pay city parking fees and baby-sitters and gasoline."

"This is terrible," said Lacy, who loved it. She turned away from me, lifting her chin and looking very serious. "We'll be back in two minutes," she said to absolutely nobody, "and Fraser will tell us what she's going to do about the tragic plight of the Lofting family."

There were calls and shouts from beyond the circle of lights in our false room as they left time for advertisement. "Lipton," I said. "The family name is Lipton."

"Got it," said Lacy. She called to the producer. "Who's my next scheduled guest, Veronica?"

"Hinson Tremont, to talk about Alzheimer's Disease," said the invisible Veronica.

"Cut him. Put him on another day. I'm running with this."

"Good idea," said Veronica. "Be sure to tell the viewers we'll keep them posted on the amount of money that comes in and we'll give credit on the air if they want it. They always like that."

"How many minutes?" I said nervously.

"Three. Can you handle it?"

I looked at the large clock on the wall beyond Lacy; its flat red second hand rushing through the advertising time. Three minutes to talk on a subject I had never considered.

Or had I?

After all, back when we decided to have a school-wide tag sale and I drew the appliance booth, there had been plenty of fund-raising suggestions that we had rejected. I sat very still, forcing myself to remember the ideas; to sift through all the possible unique ways of raising money that Mrs. Simms, the class adviser, had in her folder. She cuts them from *Woman's Day*, *Family Circle*, *Seventeen* and *Weekly Reader*.

"Okay," yelled Veronica invisibly.

"Welcome back," said Lacy, looking firmly, but sadly into the camera. She ran through the Kit situation again and turned back to me. "So what means will you utilize, Fraser, to get enough money to enable the Liptons to visit their daughter every day?"

"I think we'll have a mile of pennies," I said. "If everybody in Chapman donates their pennies, we can put together a mile."

"My goodness," said Lacy. "How much money is a mile of pennies?"

"I think it's over $800," I said. "I'll let you know when we make the 5,280th foot, Lacy." I was sure that was it. We had discarded the idea because we were aiming to make fifteen hundred dollars.

"And if that doesn't pull in all the money you need?" said Lacy.

"We'll have a road rally with clues," I told her. "We'll have an entrance fee for drivers and passengers.

We'll get the businessmen of Chapman to offer prizes. I'll ask the Chapman Savings Bank to act as trustees of the fund, and I think we can help the Liptons and have a lot of fun doing it."

"Fraser, what marvelous ideas," said Lacy throatily. She turned back to the cameras and began to give a sermon on youth today, how misjudged they are, because look at Fraser MacKendrick, a fine upstanding example of what our young people can do.

They can fake, I thought. What have I gotten myself into? On television, declaring I'll raise enough money with a mile of pennies and a road rally to help the Liptons?

Veronica, who turned out to be very young and stocky in blue jeans and a sweatshirt that said "Bronte Sisters," waved me off the set and escorted the man on Alzheimer's Disease in after all. I walked very slowly out of the studio. I went past the people who were always on the phone, as if their ears came complete with dial tone, and the whole concept sped through me.

I'll need permissions, I thought—school, bank, P.T.A., class advisers. Find someone who's done a road rally. I read about one in Wickfield once. Track that down. Figure out how to advertise for the penny mile. Figure out how to display it for progress reports. Get a committee for each. Who'll help? Smedes will. Connie will.

"I can't believe it," said Annie. Of course, we were on the phone. Sometimes I loathe Alexander Graham Bell. What right did he have to make people communicate on wires, when they need faces and gestures and intimacy?

"Well, it's true," I said. "Smedes already called and

so did Julie and Connie and even Susannah, because she and Matt broke up."

"Wow," said Annie. "I knew the powers of gossip were strong, but I didn't think word would spread that fast. But what on earth happened, Fraser? I was absolutely floored when Price told me. I can't understand it at all."

"Understand what?" I said. I flipped through my notebooks. I had a dozen more calls to make that night and forms to fill out for the bank that had agreed to keep the money for us. "You know what's really terrific, Annie? The Boys' Athletic Association agreed to run the road rally. I don't have to do any work on that at all. They've always wanted to have one and, I guess, never had the impetus to do all the work. Tim Morgan and Dick Biaggio stopped me in the hall and offered to do it for Kit. It's so *wonderful*, Annie. I didn't know there were so many good kids at Chapman High until this week."

"We're not talking about the same thing, Fraser," said Annie. "I'm talking about Michael. You dropped him. What *for*? And why didn't you call me? Why didn't you talk to me about it?"

Chapman was an enormous school. It took no effort for me and Michael to avoid each other. We knew each other's schedules and habits, so we could steer from even glimpsing each other. I would think of him when I went into fourth-period history, going into his fourth-period chemistry. I would think of him when I ate my tuna-fish sandwich at third lunch, having a hot tray at first lunch and complaining to Price about the runny gravy. When I walked past the math department, I wondered if he had rejoined Computer Club.

"It wasn't working out," I said dully to Annie.

"Yes, it was! It was working perfectly! Michael adored you, Fraser. And I know you. You adored him, too. It was all this selfish stuff, wasn't it? All those silly things you said to me about Michael consuming too much time?"

And she wonders why I didn't call her to talk about it, I thought. My explanations were nothing to her but "all those silly things."

"Fraser, how could you do this to him?" said Annie, in a voice that had despair in it. As if I had done something truly vile and she was having to cope with it. "Michael is a wonderful person. There's nobody at Chapman High as good as him. Not for you, at least. Not with your standards. So here he is in love with you and you walk out on him. *Why?*"

"I didn't do anything to him, Annie. It was *us*. I couldn't make it work, Annie. I couldn't surrender that much."

"It isn't a matter of surrendering. It's a matter of sharing," said Annie.

I began to hurt all over, as if someone had shredded my skin, like cabbage. I swallowed at the lump Annie had put in my throat. I had wept too much over Michael and me to want to start in again. Not when I had to spend the whole evening being articulate about starting up the Kit Lipton Fund.

"You're just hurting yourself," said Annie, and that much, at least, was true. I hurt terribly, and I was the one who had done it. "And you're certainly hurting Michael. Price talked with him last night. Price said he was pretty upset. And Price never talks about emotions, Fraser, so it must have been pretty bad for him even to use a word like *upset*."

That's part of it, I thought. Boys talk about electronic equipment and racing bikes and tickets to hockey games. Girls talk about children who die young. I struggled to tell Annie that, but she was disgusted with me. "Girls talk about nail-polish colors and the style of their jeans and whether to pierce their ears," she said acidly. "Give Michael a chance. He has a little sister. He'd understand how awful it is that Kit is hurt."

"He didn't understand. He only cared about driving me. About being together. Don't you see, Annie, that I'm tired of being together so much?" The last thing I wanted was a fight with Annie. I stopped myself and said, "Well, let's not bother about all that. Look, I'm really going to need some help on raising money. I know you're busy, but—"

"You are so selfish!" yelled Annie, so loudly that I cringed. "God knows, Michael gave up a lot for you. He went skiing half as much; he quit Computer Club; he rearranged his work time in order to take you places like the University Library or visiting Kit. You can't claim he didn't meet you halfway, Fraser."

"Maybe I was wrong," I said, "but even at halfway, it was too much. Michael—"

"You're not starting this fund to help Kit," said Annie in a tight vicious voice. "You're doing it because you like to be out front showing off. You're a loner, Fraser. You couldn't make a go of dating Michael because you're *selfish*, that's why. I feel as if our whole friendship was under false pretenses. You didn't need me as a friend. You just needed a co-worker in all your projects. That's the only thing you care about right now. Not Michael's feelings. Not mine. But showing off to the whole city of Chapman at how well you can raise money in a good cause."

I began crying—deep weeping, like a gray sky in

winter: hanging in there for weeks, never stopping, never lifting.

"Annie, that's not fair." I could not pull the Kleenexes out of the box fast enough to sop my tears up.

"Fair? You kick someone who loves you because he has the nerve to expect you to spend time with him and you talk about *fair*?"

We were quiet for a long time.

The tiny plastic wastebasket next to the phone was half-full of my used Kleenex when Annie said, "I have to go and practice, Fray. I'm in the orchestra for the Bach *Magnificat* the Choral Society is putting on. I didn't mean to shriek like that. I don't want to hang up mad. But I hope you come to your senses. If you really try, you could get Michael back and smooth things over."

"Thanks," I said, but I didn't feel thankful. I did come to my senses, I thought. That's why I broke up. I can't be Michael's other half. I can't design my entire life around what he wants.

Selfish, I thought. Is that what I am, really? In the end, am I simply a selfish egocentric show-off?

I could not call Michael. What would I say? I love you, but you push me to the wall? I love you, but I can't be a couple?

Chapter 11

"It turns out," said Robbie de Gennaro, "that there are eighty-four thousand, four hundred and eighty pennies in a mile, Fraser. That is a bunch of pennies. How are we supposed to display all these pennies people bring in?"

I adore Robbie de Gennaro. He's short and stocky and a super basketball player and the funniest person I have ever shared a math class with. The only trouble with him is his taste in girls. Without fail he dates some whispery giggly little creature who acts like a reject from junior high. Right now he's going around with Jodie French, who is not only whispery and giggly but also on the pompon squad. I ask you.

"Line them up along the hallways," said Smedes.

"Little tracks of pennies circling Chapman High. Little copper trains of—"

"Smedes," said Anselm Meriweather, "don't be absurd. Just because you're honest doesn't mean everybody else is. We can't have eight hundred dollars in pennies lying on the floor."

Anselm is president of the Boys' Athletic Association. I'm not even sure what kind of athletics he's in—I think track. It's just as well. I can't imagine the cheerleaders figuring out a rhythm to shout "Anselm Meriweather" to. Especially not when our cheerleaders are of the mentality of Jodie French.

"Good point," said Smedes. I could tell she felt stupid. I wanted to rescue her. I said, "It would be great if we could, Smedes. Everywhere you went, you could just bend down and add a penny and feel generous and watch it grow. But I think what we'll do is have a rain barrel outside the principal's office. The kids in Industrial Arts can remove one stave and replace it with Plexiglas so you can look in and monitor progress."

Smedes reminds me of Lacy Buckley. Smedes is quite horsey-looking, with long, large features and droopy hair, but somehow she manages to be elegant and interesting.

"How's Kit, by the way?" said Anselm.

"She's improving a little bit. She winks. She grips her mother's hand a little. She responds to stuff like pinpricks."

"*Pinpricks*?" said Smedes, horrified. "Those doctors sit around stabbing this poor little kid with *pins*?"

"Testing reflexes," said Robbie de Gennaro.

We were sitting in the student center. It's really part of the entrance foyer—a large sunny square area back behind the stairs. In winter you can hardly sit there, because icy winds come in whenever the front doors are opened, and whatever heat there is rises up the stairs. But we were moving through spring now, and the student center was comfortable. If you call ripped vinyl sofas donated by an orthodontist who turned to classier stuff comfortable.

It was Toybrary day. I felt so strange knowing that Ginny and Leigh were running it. That they had control now, and not I. They could serve apple juice or Kool-Aid or nothing at all. They laugh with the kids and set aside special toys for their special favorites, or they could just sit there, doing their homework, glancing up occasionally if someone came in.

Jodie French came lightly down the stairs. I knew it was Jodie because we could see her feet through the stair gaps. Slender legs, clad in white tights, wrapped in ballerina ribbons. Jodie always wears interesting things. Whenever I see her I feel stodgy and too tall, and dull to the core.

Jodie half danced behind the stairs into the student center with us. She has fairly long hair and she was wearing it in a very high pony tail, so that it bobbed and bounced with every step. It was like another pompon, stuck to her skull.

"What meeting is this, Robbie luv?" she said, and she sat in his lap. She sat down as if Robbie were just another piece of furniture and Robbie sat under her as if she weren't there at all.

"Kit Lipton Fund," said Robbie. He twisted to get her hair out of his eyes, but she misinterpreted his move and flounced herself so that her hair spread all over the place. Robbie sighed and shifted his whole weight to the left so he could see the rest of us.

"How do we count the pennies?" said Smedes. "You think we should put them in penny rolls every day?"

"Glad you offered," I said. "Yes. I think you should."

"Never get on a committee with Fraser," said Anselm to Robbie. "It's too dangerous."

"Then why are you here?" said Jodie.

"Because I'm not on Fraser's committee. I'm running my own committee. I'm doing the Road Rally myself." Anselm looked at me and grinned. "That way I get to delegate all *my* work, too."

Anselm and I laughed together. It felt so good— laughing with a boy. Maybe I just had a problem with Michael, I thought. Maybe I should just find another boy.

But I knew pretty well from past experience that *finding* the boy was one thing; dating him was another.

"You know," said Robbie, "I don't think the rain barrel should go near the principal's office. It should be in the cafeteria just beyond the cash register. That way people will drop in all their change from buying hot lunch or milk or dessert."

"Oh, that's a good idea!" I said happily. I scribbled a note to myself to get the dietitian's approval.

"Robbie, you don't have time for this," said Jodie. She swiveled around on his knees with a grace I envied and bent over him and adjusted his shirt to suit herself. "You're doing the Junior Prom with me."

"I am not doing the Junior Prom," said Robbie. "I am *going* to the Junior Prom. I am not doing tickets,

128

getting a band, helping with decorations or anything else, Jodie. *You're* doing that. *I'm* doing the Kit Lipton Fund."

The year I was a freshman a girl named Kathie Block was the senior in charge of the Senior Prom. She did all the work—from advertisers in the program to getting the band, from ticket sales to decoration donations. And then nobody invited her to the dance. Every time I think of that I cringe inside.

But I knew now why she didn't just ask somebody herself—ask anybody at all, just so she could go to what was her very own dance—it hurt too much.

I was not going to be in the Road Rally. Oh, sure, I could ask one of the boys. I could invite a kid I knew from the Catholic high school. I could order all the committee heads to go in one car to give myself company. I could round up a batch of girls for my car.

But if I couldn't go with Michael, I didn't want to go.

Michael's presence was very different from anyone else's. I missed him physically. Not sexually, because we really hadn't gone very far. But he was so very male that around him I felt essentially female. It was a good feeling. Now those feelings were gone completely. They ached inside me—wanting his deep voice, his larger hands, his wide chest, all of him that was male and Michael.

But I couldn't have Michael with the suffocating.

To date was to merge—like driving down the turnpike: you came in one lane, but you had to give it up. It vanished. You had to share a lane with all the other cars, and you couldn't start up a new lane. You drove together. Or you took the next exit.

"We need a mileage chart on the barrel," said Anselm. "To show how far up the mile we've come."

"By feet," suggested Robbie. "How many pennies in a foot?

"Then you'd need five thousand two hundred eighty divisions on the graph," Smedes pointed out. "A bit unwieldly, don't you think?"

"How come you're doing all this for a kid you've never met?" said Jodie. She was irritable. Probably thought we were a threat to her. What a laugh. Robbie's taste didn't run to Smedes and Fraser.

"Because she could be my daughter," said Smedes. "Or my sister. So I care about her."

"You don't have a daughter," Jodie pointed out.

I thought, How can Robbie stand spending time in her company?

"No," said Smedes, "and I probably never will. Marriage does not appeal to me. But Kit matters. I want her to live, and I want her mother to be able to visit her every day, and that's that, Jodie. Now shut up unless you can contribute something meaningful."

Robbie winked at Smedes, and he and Smedes rolled their eyes at each other. I bet he breaks up with Jodie after the Junior Prom, I thought. He's too nice to leave her stranded the way poor Kathie Block was stranded. But he's also too nice for Jodie.

We ended the meeting. Smedes and I set off for the office to get the list of clubs and churches that were willing to put school announcements in their newsletters, and so forth. "I'll do that part," said Smedes. "I did it when we were raising money to send the marching band to the governor's inaugural parade, so I know the names."

"Thanks," I said.

It was wonderful the way committees had just materialized. Unlike Toybrary—which everybody found a slightly crazy undertaking that required too much work—the Kit Lipton Fund attracted people instantly. It was exhilarating in the way that a goal is always exhilarating. And it was probably good for me, having a door open to new friendships as the door closed behind me on Michael and Annie.

But not having Annie with me was like having a limb amputated. I had never done anything without sharing the details with her. Sometimes I felt only half there.

I saw her around occasionally. She smiled at me, got chatty, and sped off to join Price.

Two weeks after that phone conversation I realized what had happened. She had forgotten.

I think it was worse than remembering. Annie had forgotten my problems, forgotten my decisions. I wanted her to ache for me, miss me, but she didn't. The friendship had fallen out the bottom, like sand in an egg timer, until there were only grains of it left. The few times I phoned her, she seemed vaguely surprised, as if she thought I had gone on to college and wasn't due home for another semester.

"You rip the lettuce," Lynn directed me. "I'll fry the bacon."

"What do I do?" asked Ben.

"You chop chives and carrots. And if you find anything else interesting in the vegetable drawer, like red cabbage or cauliflower, chop that, too." Lynn turned to me. "I loathe a boring salad," she said confidentially.

"I know what you mean," I said, although when it comes to salad, I think it's all pretty boring.

We were having a huge spaghetti-and-salad-and-garlic-bread Sunday dinner. Mom had the dining room all ready, but the whole family was in the kitchen, perched on counters, or leaning against tilting antique mirrors, gabbing. They were all struggling to stay off the topic of *Michael, where is he*? It took an extra effort for Lynn, who was dying to know the details. I ripped a little escarole and threw it in the salad bowl with the iceberg lettuce.

"Fraser?" said my mother. I glanced up. "Your father and I have been thinking," she said.

Oh, no. Here it comes. Some sort of interference or guidance.

"College," said my mother. "Dad and I always told you that you'd go to State, where all of us have always gone. The more we've considered it, the less fair that seems. We shouldn't decide anything that important for you. We have extra money this year because of my job. Of course we toyed with the idea of taking a big trip, or buying a second car. But we decided we want you to look around at other colleges and go to whatever college suits you best."

I stood there with Boston lettuce decorating my fingers and stared at her. "You mean it, Mom?"

I knew kids whose entire junior year was spent reading college catalogs. They'd start with the East Coast and work their way across the nation to California, reading every catalog from the Naval Academy to Berkeley. But I had never dipped into any of them. Choice wasn't part of it for me—I was going to State and that was that.

I felt the country unfolding like a map in the glove compartment—college by college, state by state. I could go anywhere! I thought. Big, little, country, urban, girls, coed, science, liberal arts.

"You can get in anywhere, Fraser," said my father. He was circling the kitchen, unable to stand still with all the pride in him. "With your grades? Your science work? Your community efforts? Why, I talked with Mrs. O'Mara and she agrees that any college you apply to will take you joyfully."

My brother laughed. "One thing you have to say for our parents, Fray. They've never lacked for faith in us."

I finally set the lettuce down. "My grades aren't that terrific, really, Dad. And Mrs. O'Mara is known as a complete turtle, whose grasp of colleges is nonexistent."

"That's true," said Ben. "She was dense as a blanket when I was there. We used to get into college in spite of her."

The family drifted into talk about teachers who had been there when Ben was. Twenty thousand students at State, I thought. Lecture halls with five hundred. Mile-long walks between classes. I wonder if I'd like some little liberal-arts school someplace?

"Where's Michael applying?" said Ben.

"I don't know," I told him. I got the salad dressing out of the refrigerator and shook it with more force than I usually do. What if I don't have boy friends at college? I thought. I had better not choose an all-girls school. Nobody would meet *me* at a dance and figure I was the most romantic girl on the campus.

"How about Annie?" my mother asked.

"I don't know that either."

How bizarre, I thought. My best friend. I truly don't know where she's thinking of going to college. I remember when one of my biggest fears was that Annie wouldn't write to me, because she never writes to anybody. If things keep going the way they have been, I won't even know her address a year from now.

"What happened to Annie anyhow?" said Ben. "I never see her any more."

"She's pretty tight with Price Quincy," I said. "She doesn't have much free time." Probably Annie would try to go wherever Price went, and the chances of that were good. Price could get into any college whose only requirements were breathing and paying.

"And how is Michael these days?" said Ben. I gave him a look and he looked away. He doesn't usually interrogate me. Lynn had probably assigned him to snoop.

"We broke up," I said.

"Oh, my," said my brother. He struggled to form another question, but I gave him another look and he shrugged, embarrassed, and nodded his head at Lynn. "I forgive you," I said. "Just don't let it happen again." Our eyes met—adult brother and sister, ancient quarrels over who got the bathroom first long gone, nothing left but the affection.

We sat down and Dad served the spaghetti. Lynn put so much Parmesan cheese on hers it looked like a sand dune. Michael was a cheese freak. He even sprinkled Parmesan cheese on his salad, in his soup, over his pizza. *Don't think about Michael.*

"We played bridge with the Hollanders once," said my mother. She looked at Dad for confirmation. "About ten years ago. We were in that couples tournament. You remember that, dear?"

"Vaguely." My father made a big deal of twirling spaghetti around his fork. I was very aware of him and Ben trying not to get involved in anything emotional that might come of a discussion about Michael and me.

"They were such good partners," said my mother. She leaned forward and waved her fork in my direction, and Lynn leaned forward too. They were trying to *locate* something emotional so they *could* get involved. "Mrs. Hollander brought her crochet to do when she was dummy," my mother added.

"Michael's mother is long gone," I said. "Presumably taking her deck of cards and her crochet with her. Now stop fishing, Mom. We split up, and that's that."

Dad and Ben were visibly relieved that they were not going to have to face tears and details. Lynn and Mom were irked, but before Mom could protest that she had not been fishing, that she never pried, Ben said, "So, Dad. Did you sign up for that travelogue series you were talking about a few weeks ago?"

Transparent, but it worked. "Yes," said Dad. "Tomorrow's the first film lecture. China is first. Then Japan, then India."

"The Far East?" I said, surprised. I turned to my mother. "but I thought Scandinavia was your dream. Fjords and reindeer."

"The East is where the action is," said Dad, and he rambled on about emerging economic strength.

His wanting to go to the East is enough for Mom, I thought. If he wants it, she will. It'll override her own wants.

I stared into my spaghetti. The tears came not just

135

from behind my eyes but from inside my throat, thickening it, filling my chest till it ached and throbbed with pressure.

I'll never have a boy friend again, I thought. I'll never date seriously. Never have a love affair. Never get engaged or married. No matter how much I want a boy in my life, it won't happen.

There's something wrong with me.

I can't share that much.

"Fantastic meal," said Ben contentedly. "What's for dessert?"

I swallowed at the blockage in my throat.

My mother said, "Mud pie. Fraser made it this afternoon."

Ben crowed with delight. "I knew there was a good reason to have a sister. Mud pie!"

Mud pie is the one dish I'm always willing to make. You crush chocolate wafers for the crust. Then you take softened ice cream and beat crushed cookies, crushed pecans and slivered chocolate into that. You layer it with whipped cream and top it with more whipped cream, sprinkling the last of your crumby bits on top. It's heavenly.

I got up to start clearing and bring in the mud pie. The doorbell rang.

"Front door?" said Ben. "We never use the front door. Must be Michael. Nobody else ever bothered with the front door."

Michael.

I never made mud pie for Michael. If this is Michael, I will kiss him a hundred times. I will promise to share everything always, from ice hockey to computer kills. I'll fix him the best mud pie that ever—

"Why, Mrs. Lipton," said my father at the front door. "What a pleasure. Come on in for dessert and coffee with us."

I sagged against the counter. Mrs. Lipton. Not Michael.

If you want Michael back so much, call him up, I thought. Make an effort. Start the compromises.

"Fraser dear," said Mrs. Lipton, and we did kiss, but it was about twelve inches lower and considerably less passionate than I had in mind. "I wanted you to be the first to know," she said. Her voice was quivering, but a smile decorated her face. She was no longer a worn-out old woman. She was like a little bird at the winter feeder, darting in and out. Pudgy, small, brown but bright. Definitely the mother of a Kit. "Kit had her first food by mouth today. And today she uttered her first syllable. It even made sense. She said *anks* when I fixed her pillows."

"She said *thanks*?" said my mother. "Oh, Mrs. Lipton, that's absolutely *wonderful!*" Mom came over and hugged Mrs. Lipton, and then Lynn hugged her, and the four of us hugged like a cheerleading squad and laughed with delight.

"The doctors think she's definitely going to recover most of what she lost," said Mrs. Lipton. "And Fraser, if we hadn't had the money you raised for us, we couldn't have gone to see her every day. There's no doubt she's made all this progress because we never gave up. We talked and sang and worked and struggled with her every minute of every day. So the thanks are yours, Fraser. You did it."

Then we were all crying. My father and Ben slipped away, but we women sat and talked of hospitals and doctors, of parking spaces and the number of pennies in a mile. "Men," said Lynn to me, shaking her head. "Never can stand talking about emotions and hurt."

Is that true? I thought. Is Michael the same? Did he ache for Kit the way he'd ache for Katurah, but he couldn't say that to me? All he could do was drive me to the hospital?

Oh, Michael. Did I hurt you, breaking up? And all you could say was Okay because it hurt too much to say anything else? Are you out there having a wonderful time on a date with some other girl? Or are you sitting in your basement, your computer screen blank, stereo silent, scanner off, tilted back in your chair thinking about me?

Chapter 12

"May I join you?" said Annie.

I was so delighted to see her that I was slow to answer. Smedes said, "Sure." Annie sat down next to me and we grinned at each other, as if there had never been a rift, as if we had last talked only hours before. "We're just figuring out where we stand on the Lipton Fund," said Smedes. "Whether we need to launch another project. We had such phenomenal success with the Road Rally that we could do another of those if we have to. Are you just passing through, Annie, or do you want to work with us?"

"I'm just passing through," she said. "Price has started coaching Little League. He's off rounding up his fifth-graders and I'm supposed to be filling this water jug with cold water. I was hoping you were talking about something interesting, but you're not."

"Certainly it's interesting," said Connie. "Hard work is always exciting, fascinating, intriguing. You came to the right place. We're short forty feet of a mile of pennies and somebody has to figure out how to get that last bit. Now that's interesting, Annie. Beats Little League any day. What are your thoughts?"

"Haven't got any," said Annie, laughing. She shook her head, and smiled at me again, and it was the same smile, a watermelon smile, the smile of friends, but it was no more directed at me than at Smedes or Connie. She was just in a cheery mood, and we were just there.

"Let's ask Lacy for more publicity," said Connie. "I think she'd do it. And Fraser, this time I want to go on television, too."

"Being on television is about as exciting as sitting in this student center," I said.

"You just don't want to share the thrills," said Connie. "Come on, let me go too."

"You and Robbie and Anselm and Smedes can do it all," I said. "It's definitely your turn."

"Oh, goodie," said Connie.

"Oh, *yuckie*," said Smedes. "*I'm* certainly not going on television. At least your name doesn't make people break down and laugh insanely, Fraser. Smedes? You do realize it's the name of one of the pirates in *Peter Pan*?"

"At least your name isn't boring," said Annie. "My name is the pits. Every fourth girl I meet has the same name."

"I've always wondered what makes people choose

140

the names they do," I said. "My brother went and married a perfectly nice girl named Lynn and they saddled their poor little boy with *Jake*. It's such an ugly name. Sharp and pointy."

"I wish we all had names like yours, Connie," said Smedes.

"My initials spell CAW," said Connie. "I go through my life with CAW on my luggage, like some sort of crow."

Annie giggled and countered with the initials of Price's cousin, GAG. It was so odd to have her there and know that she could be anybody at all, for all the impact she had on me on now. She was an acquaintance, but not a best friend. I waited for the pang, maybe even for tears, but they didn't come.

"Does anybody have a privateer?" said Connie.

"A what?" I said.

"A privateer."

"What on earth is that?" said Smedes.

"That's what my mother calls tampons," said Connie. "I need one."

We began laughing helplessly. "That's nothing," said Connie. "You should hear the words she uses for bowel movement and vagina."

"I think I'll pass," said Smedes. "My life is cluttered with enough stupid words. But yes, I have an extra privateer."

We kept laughing, but nicely, as if we—who didn't know Connie's mother at all—loved her nevertheless, even if she did have to call tampons privateers. We moved naturally from this into various female problems and conditions, and from there to college, and from there to the act of leaving high school and family for good.

It was girl talk. "I've missed this," I said.

"Missed what?" asked Annie.

"Girl talk."

"Fraser," said Annie, "for a liberated woman of our times, you certainly say some peculiar things. There's no such thing as girl talk."

"There is, too. Boys talk about the scores of games or the cost of car accessories, but they don't actually *talk*."

Annie gave me a look that would wither flowers.

"Like us," I said. "Like all the hours you and I talked."

"Oh, Fraser. What did we ever talk about except boys?"

I stared at her. I was wrong. She could still affect me a lot. Because we had shared a thousand things— hope, joy, triumph, failure, success, anger. Not a boy in sight. She's forgotten it all, I thought, or no longer cares.

Smedes said, "I agree with you, Fraser. Conversation is different with all girls." She began putting her things back into her purse. She had one of those purses divided into numerous zippered compartments. I always forget where I put things, or I forget that I even possess them. Smedes was far better organized. She tucked a short pencil here, a long pencil there, slipped a tiny notebook into a pocket just the right size, and whisked a tampon out of a compartment at the bottom.

"It's a lot more fun talking with boys," said Annie, thus knocking the eight years in which she had talked exclusively with me.

Smedes just laughed. "When Jim and I were dating really heavily, that was what got me the most. All that fun. I kept wanting not to be having so much fun all the time."

We all stared at her. Annie with confusion, me with excitement, Connie simply wanting the tampon. "I mean, sometimes you look at the evening ahead and you don't want to party. You don't want company. You don't want to make an effort. You want to sit alone in the front of the television eating cheese Doritos and sour cream."

I was almost holding my breath. Say more, Smedes, I thought. I can't believe you feel the way I do. I can't believe another person out there—someone I like and admire—actually agress with *me*.

"But Smedes," objected Annie, "if you feel that way, what's the point in dating at all?"

"I adore Jim. He's perfect for me. But we were suffocating each other, having all that fun. Jim kept telling me he couldn't breathe, and I felt the same. Now our relationship is semi-detached."

Connie said, "Now if I could only detach that tampon from your iron grip. If you're going to give somebody something, you should do it promptly, Smedes, and without all this fanfare."

"Semi-detached?" repeated Annie, visibly horrified. "Smedes, that sounds like a building."

"Exactly," said Smedes. She waved the tampon in the air like a cigar for congratulations. Connie caught it on to the second trip and abandoned us for the lavatory. "It is like a building, Annie. You have to build with the bricks you've got, and Jim and I decided to construct a semi-detached."

The phrase settled on my mind as if I'd been hunting for it since last November. *Semi-detached*. You share some, you separate some. How come nobody I know does that? I thought. Everyody I know is so attached they're indivisible.

Smedes turned to me and made a face. "I mean, Fraser, we're talking here about a guy whose favorite activity is arm-wrestling. I kid you not. Jim goes hundreds of miles to watch people arm-wrestle. I went once and I said, 'Hey, man, this is *yours*. I'm sticking to theater.' "

"So that's what you do?" I said. "Theater?"

"Stage work. Musicals. Soap operas on television. Shakespeare. I'm not choosy. Anything that takes acting. It's my only interest. Jim can't stand any of it."

"Well, I don't see what kind of relationship *that* is," said Annie stiffly. "You always off doing your thing and him always off doing his thing. Although I have to admit if Price's thing were arm-wrestling I would have real difficulties going along, too. But what do you do *together*?"

"We eat. I love food. Jim loves it even more. We meet exclusively at mealtime, and we eat together." Smedes began laughing. "Why, Annie, sometimes we even talk. And it must be successful, because he's taking me to the Prom next week."

She stood up to leave. She was so pleased with herself about the way she and Jim had worked things out. And so calm. That was what impressed me most. As if any clod could see that that was how you worked things. You start to drown each other; obviously, you both get out of the water.

I've been around the wrong girls, that's all, I

thought. I was with the Annie-Lynn-Mom-and-Judith crowd. I should have been with the Smedes types.

"Well, I think it's terrible," said Annie. "You're not even a couple."

"Sure we are. Just a different variety from you and Price."

Watermelon friends, I thought, looking at Smedes and not Annie. Maybe you have different ones all your life. Maybe some of them never even realize it. You get a truth from them, but they pass on. But as long as someone understands, you'll be all right.

I hardly noticed that Annie was leaving. I heard her say something about filling the water jug and I think I said goodbye, but I didn't notice. I said, "Smedes? How did you *know*? How were you *sure*?"

Smedes shrugged into her cardigan and draped her shoulder strap over it. She hoisted her books into her arms and checked around to be sure she was leaving nothing behind. "It was pretty obvious, Fraser. That kind of relationship is like ice on a windshield. You can't see a thing beyond it."

The night of the Junior Prom I sat alone in my bedroom.

It's not a romantic bedroom. It's an ordinary square room in an ordinary house, with one chest and two windows. The bed has a plain ribcord spread, the kind that lasts for years and years, although you keep hoping it's going to tear and get spoiled so you can buy something new. When you lie down, you get rippled marks on your skin.

Semi-detached, I thought.

Like a building.

But Michael isn't like Jim. Michael never admitted to being trapped. Michael never said he wanted less. He said he wanted more. How could you have a semi-detached relationship with someone who wanted to emulate Annie and Price?

I wandered around the room. Annie's room is so romantic, I thought. Look at mine. A door set on two filing cabinets for a desk. I stared at the desk. My finished report on Eliza lay on top. A-plus. "Excellent research," wrote Mr. McGrath. "The best organization I've seen in years."

I'm not good at being a girl friend, I thought. I'm not good at being a date. I'm not romantic.

Even Smedes is more romantic than I am. At least she found a boy who matched her.

And I couldn't have called Michael up before the Junior Prom and asked him to be semi-detached. It would have sounded as if all I wanted was an escort and then I'd dump him until the next interesting weekend. How could a person even *use* the term *semi-detached*?

Annie was right. It sounded like a building. Two people in love didn't talk like that.

I wanted to be at the Junior Prom.

I wanted to be a girl like Jodie, my horizon only as wide as the next boy.

I wanted to be silly and happy and pretty and flirtatious and romantic as roses.

But it would not happen. I was no Annie, whose personality could shift as music changes keys, to match the boy she chose. I was Fraser, and I was stuck with myself, and I was not good at being romantic.

Chapter 13

"How'd the interview go?" said my father anxiously.

"Not so good. I kept yawning in her face."

My father looked at me in utter disgust. He had raised me all these years so I could spend a college interview yawning?

"It was hot in there, Dad. I got sleepy. I kept trying to bite on the yawns and keep them inside my mouth, but it didn't work. My jaw cracked, and the yawns came out anyhow."

My father sighed. "Oh, well. I'm not that crazy about this college anyhow. Too small. And too feminine. All these little bushes and pretty little trees and cute little dormitories. It's not my idea of a college."

We walked back to the car. I had always thought of

college as an autumn thing. Plaid stadium blankets and autumn leaves to scuff through. But summer hung heavy over the campuses we visited. Nobody was busy. They were too hot.

"I think our first priority in college selection should be air conditioning," I told my father.

He was busy trying to find a place where we could have lunch. "The second priority should be that they have restaurants around. I can't believe how many of these colleges just squat out here in the countryside. What do they expect the parents to do? Bring picnics along?"

"I think I saw a restaurant about a half mile before we got to the campus, Dad. It was called the Four Bears, or the Six Doors, or something."

We were getting punchy. Nine colleges in four days is a lot of campuses. It was necessary to keep a notebook so we could remember one from the other.

"Just don't choose that one where the freshman girls lived in a dorm that looked like a horror-movie set," said my father. "Your mother would have a nervous breakdown visualizing you there. You'd have to major in writing occult novels."

"It wasn't that bad. Lot of stones, and dead ivy, and a broken clock on the spire." We walked over a steaming pavement to where we had parked our car. He was right about this campus. It was very girlish. I didn't feel a part of it. I felt too heavy-handed and organized and academic for this place. "I wish I were interesting," I said.

"Interesting!" said my father. "You knocked the socks off everyone who interviewed you."

"Not quite. But I meant *romantic* interesting."

He got uncomfortable and started the car up instead of discussing it. We found the restaurant, but it turned out to be a clothing store named the Four Seasons.

"Check the map," I said. "How far are we from the nearest town?"

"I'm sure we're not near any town. I had no idea this end of the state was so vacant. I don't know what happened to all this urban sprawl we keep reading about. There's nothing here but farms and colleges." He opened the map.

"We're only forty miles from State," I said. "Let's just drive down there, wander around a little, do some comparing, eat at the cafeteria, and drive on home."

"As long as you put food first," said my father, "I think I can go along with that."

We headed with empty growling stomachs for the next university. If they have good food today, I thought, I'll probably choose my school on the basis of its cafeteria. I'm starved. I'm so hungry my stomach is flapping.

"Your mother really wanted to come on this trip," said Dad. "She was heartbroken that she couldn't take the time off from work. It's lousy. She worked all her life to raise you from infancy to the moment when you'd start leading your own life, and now she's missing the special part. Seeing where you'll go, how you'll fit in."

What if I never fit in? I thought.

"It's your mother's money paying for college, you know. Her only real purpose in starting that career was to send you."

"Does she mind?" I said.

"Mind!" repeated my father. "Fraser, there's nothing she wants more in life than to have you succeed. Except maybe to go to Scandinavia."

I laughed. "But you want to go to China and India."

"That can wait. When we get you through college, your mother and I will hit Norway."

"You shouldn't wait four years," I said. "I can go to State, and it won't cost that much, and you can go this year."

We were there. My father drove around the campus, the way he always does, past his old fraternity house, past the playing fields, past the building that was the entire engineering department when he was there and is now a tiny wing. Past the vast student center that always appalls him because it was paid for by alumni and he thinks it's too grandiose.

So, he understands that she wants Norway more than he wants China, I thought. Maybe what it is is that each couple has to find out what kind of pair they are. Semi-detached or fully intertwined, or anything else. As long as it works.

We got out of the car and walked up stone steps worn smooth by a hundred years of student feet. A few students from summer session were walking slowly across the grass. Several were lying under oak trees, spread-eagled to cool off, and one art class was sketching, except for the two class members who were napping.

"Twenty thousand kids here," said my father. "A few of them have to be suitable, Fray. Somebody out there is going to think you're 'romantic interesting.' "

He actually said it, I thought. Referred to my social and emotional status.

We were only steps from the cafeteria when my father took my arm, almost harshly, as if to stop me from doing something dangerous. "Sweetheart," he said in a strange voice, "you can go where you want. Truly, any place on the globe comes second. Your mother and I want the best school for you. It probably isn't State. Don't come here just because it's easy. Don't come here just because it's familiar. *Do what's right for you.*"

We stared at each other. My father's eyes seemed to mist over, but maybe not. He turned and entered the cafeteria swiftly.

The cafeteria was vast. Several of the larger dormitories have their own cafeterias, but this one is also open to the public. It has two lines: the cheap one for soup, sandwiches, Jell-O and potato-chip packages, and an expensive one with as many choices of casserole, salad and meat as a cruise ship.

I can go anywhere, I thought. He promised. It matters more to Mom than anything. It's what she's working for.

Me.

I took a fork, knife and spoon. I took a heated plate, set them on the tray and began sliding it down the buffet rack.

As many colleges to choose from as dishes in the buffet, I thought. All different textures, flavors, varieties.

"Well, I'll be darned," said my father, slipping his

wallet back into his pocket as we left the cashier. "Look who's waving to us from across the room."

I glanced over, expecting to spot some old alum he remembered from thirty years ago, but it was not. It was Mr. Hollander.

And Michael.

A good thing I had had practice making difficult walks. Like going to see the Liptons at the hospital waiting room. Walking toward Michael was the hardest thing I had done all summer. Any poise, any casualness I had acquired from visiting all those colleges left me. I was just an awkard high-school girl, stumbling toward a boy she had dumped.

"Hi there," said my father, delighted. He and Mr. Hollander shook hands. "Michael here for an interview? Hi, Michael." My father shook hands with Michael too. I just stood there with a heavy tray in my hands and tried to smile normally.

Michael looked appealing as ever. He was still lovely.

Lovely. Funny word to use for a boy. But he was, to me. I thought, I could fall back into you the way Kit toppled downstairs. Forever. Finally. And it might even be worth it. I said, "Oh, hi, Michael. How are you?"

He shoved his own tray down to make room for mine. I sat down opposite him. "Never saw you eat that much," said Michael, looking at my loaded plate. "College interviews really require stoking up, huh?"

"I didn't know you wanted to come here," I said.

"I don't know what I want to do. Dad and I are looking at everything."

His voice caught at me. Deep. Warm. Our fathers talked about colleges as if *they* were the ones about to attend. Majors, admission requirements, tuition increases.

Michael said, "So how's Kit?"

He had a funny smile on his face. He's asking that right off, I thought, so I can't accuse him of being thoughtless. I smiled back, but my smile was embarrassed, awkward. "She's better. They're going to be able to bring her home in August and do out-patient therapy."

"That's great," said Michael. He looked at his empty plate and then at my full one. "You really going to eat all that?"

"Probably not. You want some?"

"That turkey really looks good."

I gave him the turkey.

"I was proud of you," said Michael, his mouth full of turkey. "Throwing yourself into raising money for Kit. I liked the mile of pennies."

"You gave to it?" I said.

"Every week I put a roll in. That didn't really add up to much money. So I bought a Road Rally seat for twenty-five dollars instead of five."

"Your name wasn't on the list!" I cried. "I'd have seen it. I checked them all, just to see if—"

Michael grinned so widely his whole body seemed to be participating in it. "Just to see if I did?" he said.

My father said, "Well, we didn't go there. It seemed pretty out of the way to me."

Michael's father said, "It *is* out of the way. They're *all* out of the way. But I'm told they have an excellent botany department and I know Fraser was quite a botany expert."

"No, I wasn't," I said. "I just did an experiment that didn't work out too well but looked impressive."

"That's half of life," said Mr. Hollander, laughing.

Michael said, "You want to take a walk around the campus with me, Fraser?"

It's a huge campus. You could walk for hours and still find sidewalks you hadn't used, dorms you hadn't noticed. I said, "Sure."

We walked everywhere. We talked about college subjects—where we'd find part-time jobs; whether we'd like freshman English; what to do if you don't like your roommate.

"I missed you," I said.

We were standing in the middle of an enormous graveled area filled with large inexplicable modern sculptures. They seemed to have cutting edges, and whatever they were intended to mean, they were sure of themselves. It made me sure to be among them. I would tell Michael how I felt. I would tell him about Smedes and Jim. About being semi-detached.

"I missed *you*," he said.

We were still walking, threading among the sculptures. "It wasn't that you weren't perfect," I told him. "It was that it was too much. Too much of a good thing. I started to drown in all that we did together."

Michael stared at me. "Too much?"

"I guess I'm not very romantic, Michael," I said, and the urge to be truthful began to hurt inside, because it sounded so stupid, so dull. Keep going, I thought, you can't stop now. "I loved you, but I didn't love spending all my time in a pair. There were other people. Other things to do." I was beginning to cry. Damn tears! "I'm sorry," I said, and I was done. I couldn't

154

have added another syllable if he begged me for it; I had choked myself already.

"It wasn't me?" said Michael. "It was us?"

"Sort of."

"You might have tried explaining that to me before. I figured you wrote me off because I was this creep who didn't care if little girls died of head injuries."

"It wasn't that!" I cried. "I just needed more—I don't know—room around me than Annie seemed to. I couldn't share that much. It was terrible. I felt so selfish. I just took it out on you, Michael, but it was my character that didn't work out. Not yours."

"Oh, Fraser, why didn't you just *say* so? How do you think I felt? I had to quit Computer Club when I was getting ready to teach my first course. I had to give up skiing half the only snowy weekends of the whole winter. I had to change my whole life to fit you in."

It's going to happen right here, I thought. We'll break up all over again; we'll cut ourselves on those metal sculptures; we'll burn each other. So much for truth.

"I wanted to," said Michael. "I wanted you to be in everything I was. It seemed to work so well for Price and Annie. I couldn't figure out why it wasn't working for us."

"Smedes and Jim are different. They're semi-detached."

"They're what?" said Michael. "That sounds like an apartment."

I explained it to him.

"I don't like that phrase," said Michael flatly.

Why are we doing this to each other? I thought. He doesn't quite understand what I'm saying, I don't quite understand what he's saying. You can't be *any* kind of attached unless you understand each other.

"I like semi-*at*tached," said Michael. He grinned at me and put his arms around my waist and swung me around. I had forgotten that he was so much taller and heavier than I. "Half of me wanted to give up everything for you, Fraser," he said, "and half of me wanted to give up *nothing*."

"I know those halves," I said ruefully.

He was holding me too closely for me to see clearly. I pulled back and squinted in the blazing sun, and I could see him. Perhaps it was the first time I really did see him. A person with his own life, whose gears couldn't mesh with mine that often. But when they did mesh, it would perfect.

"Senior year starts in a month," said Michael.

Senior year? I thought. It was actually a surprise to realize there was still a year of high school left. I had been thinking college, college, all summer, thinking freedom, independence, change. "Do you have lots of plans?" I said to Michael.

"Yes. You?"

"Likewise."

We were still walking. The sculptures receded. One of the few remaining elms on campus loomed ahead, its symmetry startling, its shade altogether appealing. But the shade was already taken by three couples.

"We could try it," said Michael, smiling at me. His smile was rather shy, as if he too wanted to walk carefully into another relationship.

"Semi-detached, you mean?" I said.

"Semi-*at*tached, I mean."

"I can't be your other half, Michael."

"Nor I yours," he said.

We will be friends, I thought. Sometimes we'll be in love, and sometimes we'll be too busy to remember. Annie would call it selfish. Smedes would call it sane.

"I call it a good idea," I said, and we sealed it with a kiss.